Ski

An

Translated by Jacky Collins

Published by Corylus Books Ltd

Skin Deep is first published in English the United Kingdom in 2023 by Corylus Books Ltd, and was originally published in Spanish as *Llevar en la piel* in 2023.

Corylus Books Ltd

corylusbooks.com

ISBN: 978-1-7392989-0-6

1

Written on the Body

Inspector Canonne was not having a good day. Dental implants that worked for everyone else were just not working for him. After waiting for several months to have it put in, two weeks later it had to be taken out, because the pain it caused him was unbearable.

'It's unusual, but sometimes it does happen,' his dentist told him brusquely. 'There are some bodies that are unable to accept them. We'll have to explore other options.'

Just as in a police investigation that's going nowhere; giving up on other options... the worst prognosis.

'Yes, I understand. A false tooth with its plastic base to fit on the gum.'

'It's not plastic, Inspector. It's resin,' the dentist retorted. 'And it looks fine.'

But it's got to be noticeable when you're kissing, thought Canonne, although he didn't say so. His dentist didn't seem like an expert in kissing.

He hadn't kissed Laure much during the days they'd finally been able to spend together. How was it possible to kiss with a mouth that was hurting so much before the extraction and bleeding at the slightest touch after? But that wasn't the real reason, and Cannone knew it only too well. And she'd left that very same morning, very early, to go back to her house, her world. Of course, Laure didn't say 'her' but 'my' – my house and my world.

Summer for couples was like having dental implants: for the majority it all went well, they filled in the gaps, tightened anything that was slack, wobbly, about to fall. But once again, that hadn't worked for him, and Laure had gone back much earlier than planned, without any breakfast.

'I'll get something on the way. I've a long journey ahead.'

And the Inspector thought she wasn't thinking about the road back home, but rather the removal of the implant that he represented, and that Laure's body had rejected.

He felt around the wound with his tongue and felt a stabbing pain and the rusty taste of blood. In any case it was turning out to be an awful summer; a detestable combination of cold, wind and rain that meant no going to the beach, so angry people, frustrated at having their holidays spoiled, filled the streets, bars and shops in the centre and forced the police to be called out constantly, most of the time for the slightest nonsense.

So the Inspector was in a foul mood when Deputy Inspector Frier, who had no dental problems and presumably no relationship troubles either, came into his office and informed him of the discovery.

'We've just had a call. They've found the body of an elderly woman in a holiday apartment in Biarritz. It would seem she's been murdered in quite macabre circumstances. We've notified the Forensics Team.'

The body had been discovered by the owner of the property when she went to pick up the keys the client should have left on the hallway table before twelve o'clock, as they'd agreed.

*

'I'm Inspector Canonne of the Bayonne Criminal Investigation Team and this is Deputy Inspector Frier. So, Mrs...'

'Moulier.'

'You're the one who found the body.'

'That's correct.'

'I hope you haven't touched anything.'

'Of course not. Well actually, yes, there was something.'

'So, did you, or didn't you?'

'As soon as I went into the apartment, I switched off the air conditioning right here, look, right next to the door. They had put it on full blast and the weather was freezing. And don't get me started on the bill. You have no idea what these renters can get up to...'

'Can we continue?'

'Thank goodness we asked them for a deposit.'

The Inspector got the impression, from the owner's reaction, that she regretted having mentioned the deposit straightaway, knowing she would probably have to pay it back. He stuck his tongue again in the empty socket, his upper first premolar, so visible at the front of his mouth.

'Apart from the aircon, have you touched anything else?'

'Nothing, I swear. I didn't even go into the bedroom. The door was open and from the doorway I could see the woman lying on the bed in a terrible state. Then I left the apartment straight away. I've watched crime dramas and I know what to do, and more importantly, what not to do. So, without wasting any more time, right away, I called you.'

Canonne put on latex gloves, went in the bedroom and approached the bed where a naked elderly woman lay, her body badly marked.

'Where's the pathologist?'

'We've already contacted him, don't think he'll be long getting here,' replied DI Frier.

The Inspector was deeply disturbed. Perhaps because what he was seeing on the bed in front of him wasn't just a dead body, but an elderly body, in all its stark, naked reality. He searched around in his mouth for the stitches. He hadn't been bothered about going bald, or seeing lines appear on his face, but this tooth thing he just couldn't stand. Because the hole in his mouth seemed like an entrance door; and he could see himself on the threshold of old age, just like he was now stood before the corpse of the disfigured old woman.

'Where is the pathologist?'

'He's on his way.'

Canonne shivered. It was still cold in the flat. Outside as well. The end of summer brought with it an urgency that caused the beaches to empty out and the streets to fill with disappointed holidaymakers looking for something to make their stay feel worthwhile. This murder was going be the highlight of the season. All the elements for a spectacular end of season party were right there, laid out on that ordinary bed fitted with cheap sheets.

The pathologist was a young man that Inspector Canonne had never worked with before. He took this fact as bad omen. It only took a simple glance at the body to realise that this was no case for a beginner.

'Doctor Ferran, François Ferran.'

'Inspector Canonne.'

While the doctor examined the body, Canonne went out on to the landing and called the Public Prosecutor's office.

'This looks bad,' he said. 'A murder that as well as being gruesome is "sophisticated"; we're really going to get it in the neck from the press if the details of this get out... Yes, the pathologist is here, a young man, Ferran, he's new to me... Well, I hope he's extremely competent, as you say, because this is complicated... Yes, the forensic team is here... OK, we'll wait for you to get here.'

The Inspector didn't tell the prosecutor that he hadn't liked Ferran as soon as he'd laid eyes on him, the reason being he'd turned up dressed like he was going to a cocktail party and not a crime scene. What galled him most was that Ferran seemed to have a disgustingly perfect set of teeth.

'The fact that the body has been lying in a room where the temperature is so low makes it difficult to assess time of death,' said the pathologist in a ridiculously stiff medical way, 'but after the nominal analysis that I've just carried out and pending the verdict of the autopsy...'

Inspector Canonne offered an ironic smile, the kind given through closed lips. Just what we need right now, he thought, another bored summer visitor in search of a show.

'She's been dead around ten hours, which means that the murder took place between three and five early this morning.'

A particularly gruesome murder. The victim was totally naked, lying face up, her face, neck, arms and stomach covered in bizarre burn marks. These had been produced, according to the forensics officer's first impression by a potent, highly corrosive acid.

'Most probably sulphuric, given the corrosion caused to the body and the vapour still hanging in the air. But we'll have to wait...'

'For the autopsy,' said the Inspector.

The pathologist didn't seem to capture the irony in Cannone's words, in fact on the contrary he seemed to take it as a compliment because he quickly qualified what he'd said by adding, 'In that case let me just say 'confirmation' of the autopsy. The more I look at the wounds, the more convinced I am that it was sulphuric acid. And the acid has been applied with great "care", if you'll allow me to put it like that, and of course after death.'

'How can you be so certain that she was already dead?'

'Inspector, please, you don't seem new to this kind of situation, a rookie, as it's normally called.'

Where had this arrogant pup come from, all dressed up like a fashion advert, talking like an old pedant and who felt it was all right to treat him like a novice? He'd more than twenty years' experience behind him. Yet the pathologist was totally wrong; suddenly Cannone felt like an absolute beginner with no experience and more than anything with no control, with an urge to grab the doctor by the lapels of his preppy jacket and to put him in his place without further ado. And all because of that damn tooth; because he'd always been the kind who was quick to open his mouth but now he did it with the same precautions as someone opening a prison door. His first upper premolar, so upfront, so visible. The caution was driving him mad. So he searched Frier's face for a sign of solidarity and caught his breath.

Then he returned to look at the body, a scenario that the medical officer knew how to interpret much better that he did.

'Doctor Ferran, let's get things straight,' he said. 'The rookie in this context is you.'

'If you say so.'

'Let me explain, so that you can get used to the way we do things round here. How it normally works is that you answer my questions clearly, no frills, no fuss, so that Inspector Frier, who's over there by the door, not bothering anyone – she is so discreet in every way to the extent that I bet you haven't even noticed her – so that she can take notes and, thus contribute to solving this terrible matter as soon as possible. So, I ask you once more, can we confirm that this woman was dead when she was burned with acid?'

Ferran's response sounded conciliatory, almost submissive.

'Without a doubt, Inspector. Not only is there no blood on the bed...'

Did acid burns usually bleed if the victim was alive? The Inspector didn't know, he'd never come across a case like this before. Yet, this type of injury was on the increase everywhere, also in Europe. And the victims were always women, as was the case here.

'But what really helps me draw that conclusion is the look on her face.'

'Well, what remains of it.'

'There's enough, Inspector. The eyes, nose, mouth are all intact... More than enough to understand that she didn't seem to have suffered from contact with the acid. Her features reflect a calmness. When the murderer poured the acid, this woman was sleeping soundly, dying or already dead, killed with a generous dose of poison. A benign substance, which neither hurts nor causes the body to convulse. A massive dose of morphine, for example. It's normally found around the elderly.'

'Could she have been dressed at the time of death?' Frier asked, coming close to the bed.

When he heard her deep voice, more typical of a big burly man than such a fragile looking woman, the doctor jumped and blushed straight away, as if they had suddenly applied a salmon-coloured mask over his face from chin to forehead.

Inspector Canonne didn't smile, he was thinking about Laure, but he said to himself, by way of comfort, that Ferran was too impressionable to have chosen the profession of forensic pathologist for himself. Rather, someone, somewhere was pulling his strings.

'What would you say, Detective?'

'If the murderer had undressed her after death, if they had moved and tampered with the body, would they have been able to leave that expression of peace, of assurance I would say, that is so evident on her face?'

Deputy Inspector Frier was right, as was usually the case. The key to the case probably lay in the fact that the body was naked, along with the peaceful look of the face. If the woman had undressed herself and willingly lain down on the bed, the nature of the relationship she had with the murderer seemed clear – a loving or sexual relationship. Although the age of the victim might suggest that this hypothesis be ruled out immediately. But if the murderer had undressed her after she was dead, then the range of possible suspects could be infinite.

'Is there anything that might suggest sexual relations before or after death?' the Inspector asked.

'I would need to examine the body more carefully to be able to answer you on that. But from what I have seen so far, I would say not.'

'Well doctor, carry on with the examination. The crime scene investigator is here to assist you. The prosecutor should be here soon. We'll ask for an autopsy of course and we'll need your report as soon as possible.'

ANTONIA LASSA

'It will take two days at least.'

'You'll need to work faster than that. This isn't just any old case, as you can see. Or maybe ask some of your more experienced colleagues for assistance.'

Inspector Cannone had forced this last phrase out, like someone forcing a lock, to curb the forensic pathologist's arrogance. But he didn't achieve the desired effect.

'As far as I can see, Inspector, we're all going to need help.'

A positively unbearable individual. Canonne was about to reply, but Frier, who had left the room called to him from outside and showed him her mobile as if to let him know that this was a call he had to take.

'As soon as possible, Doctor. I don't have to keep going on about this, because it's easy to see that we are not dealing with a typical case here.'

The two detectives went out on the landing.

'Who called me, Frier, the prosecutor?'

'No, no-one, but I was getting bored watching you two competing to see whose was the longest.'

'Says you with that gravelly voice of yours.'

'Well, you know me.'

In other circumstances the Inspector would have smiled.

*

The autopsy report confirmed that wealthy octogenarian Elisabeth Audiard, resident in Paris, had been murdered on 28th August at approximately four AM with a lethal intravenous dose of morphine. Her killer had burned her with sulphuric acid after she was dead. They had poured the liquid slowly and carefully over the body, drop by drop, presumably by means of a glass pipette.

'Is it easy to get hold of those glass droppers, doctor?'

'Yes, Inspector, quite easily. They can be obtained from anywhere selling laboratory equipment.'

'How slow was the administering of the acid?'

'The killer would have needed thirty minutes,' replied the forensic pathologist.

'How careful would they have needed to be?'

'Rather than being a liquid, as laymen tend to think, sulphuric acid is more viscous. It can be applied so that it comes out slowly, drop by drop, as is the case here, in my opinion.'

'Drop by drop, and we might say following a previously devised path.'

'Exactly, Inspector, following a well-devised plan. You are up against a patient, calculating individual. And if I may suggest, we're looking at someone who is, or who thinks they are, an artist.'

'Are you a psychologist in your free time, Dr Ferran?'

'I'm studying to be one. And I'm convinced by the idea I've just put forward. Someone who thinks they're an artist. What they have done on the victim's body is drawing.'

What Ferrran was saying wasn't that crazy. The acid hadn't been thrown in some haphazard way across the victim's body, rather it had been poured carefully, as if to stick to the outline of a pattern, a design the meaning of which was still impossible to establish, consisting of a centimetre-wide strip that circled the woman's face like an old-fashioned photo frame. The strip followed the contours of the face perfectly, starting on the forehead along the hairline and coming down on either side just in front of the ears. In the bottom half of the face, it followed the jaw line, covering the chin completely. Two more strips of a similar width could also be seen on either side of the neck. And two strips, a little wider, went from top to bottom on the inside of the arms. Lastly, a more important strip, around three centimetres wide, crossed the old woman's stomach, from one side to the other, just above the pubis.

'If you'll allow me, and it helps your investigation in some way, I'd suggest you look for someone with artistic aspirations,' repeated the pathologist.

'And the strip they have traced across her pubic region is, without a doubt, their signature. Just like someone signing a painting. A broad, bold signature as well. Their personality speaks of someone meticulous and narcissistic, without a doubt.'

This elderly millionairess had checked in, as every year, to the best hotel in Biarritz to spend most of the summer. So, what was she doing in that ordinary, low-end apartment that she'd reserved herself quite openly?

The owner had confirmed that point.

'Yes, yes, Inspector, she made the reservation herself by telephone and paid in advance by credit card, as I asked her to do.'

'How long did she make the reservation for?'

'Just for the one night. I handed her the keys myself on 27th August around four in the afternoon. She was to leave them on the table in the entrance hall the following day before noon, as I've told you. We don't normally accept such short stays at this time of the year, but with the terrible summer we're having and all the cancellations...'

'Did she seem anxious or worried when you saw her?'

'No, she was very pleasant and seemed perfectly calm.'

'How many copies of the key to the apartment did you let her have?'

'Just one.'

The one the police had found in the woman's handbag, along with her purse, which was untouched. The rest of the contents in the bag were all in order too. They could rule out theft as motive for the murder. Nor were there any signs of forced entry. The murderer had been let into the apartment willingly by the victim.

'I don't suppose there are any security cameras or similar surveillance devices in this building?'

'No, Inspector. What for? It's never been necessary. It's a peaceful property, as you can see. And respectable. It's the first time... What's going to happen now?'

'We'll seal the apartment off for now until we have finished the searches.'

'Will it take long?'

'As long as necessary. But afterwards you can claim compensation.'

The woman hesitated for a moment and then asked, 'And our reputation?'

Cannone was about to reply – it'll probably be good for business – but he refrained. Irony required the kind of energy that he just did not have at that moment. He looked around; this apartment was deemed a 'tourist let', but from the window there was no view of the sea, no patch of the garden, nor anything like it. All you could see were some old, ugly buildings... no, worse than that... sad, old, ugly buildings. The flip side of this elegant city. And yet, it was in this place where that rich woman, a frequent guest at the Hôtel du Palais, had died slowly and meticulously at the hands of an artistic assassin. And to top it all off, he was painstaking to the extreme. The pathologist confirmed straight away that the killer had left no traces whatsoever, no DNA evidence of having been at the scene of the crime. This investigation was going to be like climbing a wall without any toe or fingerholds, thought Canonne.

'Doctor, is it difficult to get hold of sulphuric acid?'

'No, Inspector.'

'Is it difficult to transport?'

'Not too difficult, no.'

'And to use it?'

'No, it's enough to take a few basic precautions – use some ordinary gloves, latex for example, a mask, glasses to protect the eyes and a simple glass dropper.'

'Is that sufficient to carry out something like this?'

'Yes. And you need a steady hand.'

The killer hadn't trembled at all. This investigation was going to be particularly difficult for the police. They had no clues and what's more they were going to be working under pressure. They had received the order to give this case the utmost priority.

'I have informed the investigating judge that this is a particularly repugnant and macabre crime,' said the public prosecutor. 'But there's something else, Inspector.'

And he repeated multiple times that the victim belonged to a family of 'considerable importance'.

'Giants in the agri-food industry, Canonne, with friends in very high places, as you can probably imagine.'

'I understand.'

'In France and beyond.'

Nevertheless, that "remarkable" woman made and received very few calls. No more than five names appeared in the contacts list on her mobile: her son, two friends, her hairdresser and the woman who worked as her secretary and housekeeper. In any case, apart from the last two, the others hadn't been used in the last few months. The police eliminated these five straight away from the list of possible suspects. They all had watertight alibis for the day of the murder.

Also saved in Madame Audiard's mobile were several numbers of different commercial businesses and firms: hotels – all prestigious, which reinforced even more the inconsistency of the apartment in Biarritz; taxi companies, restaurants, and luxury caterers.

But the call log also revealed two unknown numbers. The victim had called the first one twice a month, from the 7th January to 17th June, which meant two months with no connection. The second number had called her three times on the eve of the murder. Inspector Cannone and Deputy Inspector Frier looked at that unknown number expectantly, as if it held a pleasant surprise for them.

'Three calls on 27th August,' said the Inspector, 'the last one at 11pm.'

'She should have been in the apartment by then,' responded the detective enthusiastically. 'And surely still alive at that point.'

'It's too soon to get excited about this, but we may just have something here. If she answered that call so late it's because she knew the person on the other end of the phone.'

'And that person called her to arrange to meet up.'

'Yes, indeed, Frier, and she agreed to meet them in the apartment she'd rented. A discreet, if not secret, rendezvous. Otherwise, why had she chosen that property so far from the centre of Biarritz and her hotel?'

'So that number could easily belong to the killer.'

'It's quite possible,' replied the Inspector, allowing himself to be carried along by his officer's enthusiasm.

'And we know that the victim knew them, at least enough to open the door to them.'

'According to the pathologist's report, sexual relations didn't take place. But it says that, given the state of her vagina, it can't be ruled out that this woman had engaged in certain sexual activity until the end of her life.'

'That's not bad for eighty years old.'

'Well, now we've got a good lead to follow. A telephone and perhaps a lover, and I'd love to see what he looks like.'

But the initial enthusiasm didn't last long. They weren't able to gather anything from the lead that had seemed so promising. The number belonged to a pre-paid phone, acquired some months prior to the murder in a bar in Biarritz. An establishment without CCTV that was frequented on a daily basis by a countless number of people. In this, as with every other aspect, the killer seemed to have planned things very well.

'They sell a lot of these phone cards,' the owner of the bar informed the police. 'Just today I have sold eleven new ones and topped up more than a dozen as well. People talk so much on the phone, something I'm not complaining about, as you can imagine. And with the bad weather at the moment, more people are coming into the bar since they're not going to the beach.'

'I see, but according to the phone provider the card in

question was purchased in March. I suppose you don't remember who could've bought one then.'

'Impossible, Inspector, too much time has passed. And all the customers look alike, if I can put it like that. Let's say that at the rate they're in and out of the bar, you only really focus on the sale. You hardly look at the customers, unless there's something that makes them stand out, either something wonderful or really bad – something inappropriate or the complete opposite, a special kindness.'

Clearly, whoever had bought that card hadn't been distinguishable in any way whatsoever, at least not at that moment. They had paid in cash and had waited six months to activate it.

The phone provider also confirmed to the officers that, once these cards were activated, they could be used for two weeks without needing to be registered.

'Once that time is passed, Inspector, if the client doesn't send in their personal details, the line is suspended first and then cancelled.'

'So, anyone could purchase one of these cards, make as many calls as they like...'

'Until the credit runs out.'

'And once it's run out, throw the card away or destroy it.'

'Exactly.'

The operator couldn't help them work out either where those crucial three calls had been made from on the eve on the murder.

'It's what we call a burner phone, Inspector, ones that leave no trace, because they're not registered to anyone. Most probably, a very basic phone or old model, without GPS.'

A phone which the killer had got rid of straight away, extremely carefully.

The detectives turned their attention to the second anonymous number in the victim's contact list. The last call had been two months ago, which seemed to put this call out of the scope of the murder. But it was also a number that was connected to a pre-paid card, that the old woman had called regularly over the course of six months. The police now knew that to be able to keep the same number for so long, the user had to have registered their details, and topped up the card more than once.

Indeed, it was registered to an Émile Gassiat, a young man, twenty-six years old, living in Arcachon, who became the prime suspect the moment he was identified. More than anything because from this number the lad was in regular contact with another woman. She was also in her eighties, extremely wealthy and from Paris, and the police would contact her immediately.

It appeared that the motive for the murder was not robbery. But given the kind of relations suggested by these phone calls, and by the scene of the crime, there were many sordid reasons, the Inspector said to himself hopefully.

'It's all about a gigolo then?' The public prosecutor asked Cannone.

'It would appear so, yes.'

'Just what we needed. And connected to that "remarkable" woman. And also, she's not the only one. For now, we know that this lad was in a relationship with a second woman, Irène Duroudier, also from Paris and this same "type", if I may use that word.'

'Elderly, millionairess, powerful.'

'Exactly. And it's possible that there could be more victims.'

'From the same background.'

'It's quite possible.'

'I'm going to ask for the warrant right now so that we can arrest that man and question him as soon as possible.'

2

The Sound of the Sea

Émile Gassiat sails at nightfall. The weather's not the best for putting out to sea; a strong wind's blowing that feels more like winter than the end of summer. And he's not as seasoned a sailor as his mother. But he's ventured forth despite everything, because he needs to go back to it one more time. Although it's most likely that tonight he won't get anything; because tonight the roar of the wind covers the sound of the sea; and the waves are sticking to the sides of the Hirondelle as if they were made out of something else, like canvas sacks full of stones.

He's anxious, gripping the tiller which looks like it's about to give way. But it doesn't. And he isn't going to either; he's going to reach that precious spot once more; he knows perfectly well the course to chart, and the exact coordinates. He's anchored there many nights in a row.

He shouts words of encouragement to himself, one of the many pieces of advice given to him by his mother – 'head to sea', if you're going to weather the storm. He cries out once more, as if he weren't alone, but with an invisible someone helping him to stay 'head to sea'. 'I am', he replies out loud.

He's close now. He'll soon be able to drop the anchor, set up the recording equipment and get ready to spend the night awake, alert, filled with the hope that he might hear or even manage to record that unique sound that he heard a few weeks ago for the first time. Since then, this sound has gripped him like a revelation or wise advice. 'Head to sea'. Now he knows that his music, the true music he will compose one day is going to be born there. It is already contained, sensed, anticipated inside that sound of the sea.

The sound the sea makes appears to contradict itself, because it sounds like the voice of still water amid a storm-churned sea. A peaceful body of water and yet with the ability to reverberate, to make itself heard far and wide. Émile uses a different adjective each time he describes that sound – experimental, hollow, original, wild, pure, from the dawn of time.

And now, to calm his uneasiness and bolster his confidence, he goes through those adjectives again, holding fast to the *Hirondelle's* tiller, while keeping the boat on its course despite everything. 'First, wild, pure, original...'. When repeating those adjectives, one after the other, they didn't seem different. Quite the opposite. They all pointed in the same direction; in their own way, each one spoke about a beginning. They all drove him to imagine a pure music, with no memory attached, no impressions from a previous time. A music like sand untouched by human feet. He wants to reach that sound once more. That night, above the fear and the storm, he needs to hear it, record it. 'Head to sea', he shouts again. 'I *am*,' comes the response.

*

The police arrived at Émile Gassiat's home at dawn. The group was made up of officers Massé and Roland from the French gendarmerie based in Arcachon, who accompanied Inspector Canonne and Deputy Inspector Frier, appointed by the Bayonne prosecutor's office to lead on the case.

Located a stone's throw from the beach and the small fishing port of Aiguillon-Sur-Mer, the place where Gassiat lived was quite ordinary, but well-maintained. He lived on the third floor, flat B. Detectives Frier and Massé remained outside the building, covering the entrance. There was no lift. The other two officers quietly climbed the stairs up to the flat, Inspector Canonne hanging back a little while the other officer knocked on the door... once, twice, to no avail.

'Open up, police!' he called at the third knock.

Then the door opposite opened wide, and a man over sixty, dressed in a grey cotton tracksuit and on crutches, appeared in the hallway.

'If you're looking for Gassiat, don't bother to keep on knocking, because he's not in. By the way, why are you looking for him?'

'Good morning, Mr...' responded officer Roland.

'Artigues; André Artigues.'

'Do you live here, Mr Artigues?'

'For more than thirty years.'

'And how do you know your neighbour isn't home?'

'Because I heard him close the door to his flat last night. These walls are paper-thin. Then, I went to the window, and I saw him leave the building from the main entrance.'

'How do you know he still hasn't come back?'

'Because when he goes out to sea, he usually comes back much later the following day. And in any case, I'm a really bad sleeper because of the pain in my legs, you've no idea... and I would have heard him if he had come back earlier. You can hear everything here... you've no idea.'

'Especially if you've got your ear pressed up against the door,' Inspector Canonne was about to say, but he managed to hold his tongue. This indiscreet neighbour seemed to be a mine of useful information and he didn't want to rub him up the wrong way. With the agreement of the local police, he had been entrusted with the direction the investigation was taking, so Canonne moved forward and stood in Artigues' doorway. The latter took a few steps back and was once again inside his flat.

'I'm Inspector Canonne, of the Police Nationale. If it's OK

with you, I'd like to ask you some questions.'

'What has that lad done?'

'You said that when he goes out to sea, he comes back later the following day. How do you know he went out to sea?'

'I can't be certain, because from my window you can't see the moorings at the port, but he was carrying the rope and the large black canvas bag that he takes every time he goes out in the boat.'

'What do you know about the boat? Is it Gassiat's?'

'Yes. it's an old Estéou power boat that he inherited from his parents. It's good for going out on short fishing trips, but not much more. He won't have dared go far, especially with last night's storm. He won't be long coming back. What has that lad done?'

'You say the boat was inherited. So that means his parents are dead?'

'Yes, both at the same time. and they were so young. It seems it was an accident.'

Detective Roland must have felt his pulse quicken at the same time as Canonne because he approached the Inspector and gave him a look.

'What do you mean by "it seems"? What type of accident are we talking about? Something out of the ordinary or strange?'

'No, no, Inspector. I didn't express myself well. I'm talking about an everyday traffic accident. A drunk driver who went through a red light.'

'How long ago was this?'

'Four years ago.'

'From what I can see, you must have a very good relationship with your neighbour to know so much about him.'

'No, not at all. Neither good nor bad. What I mean is that he didn't give me this information. I should tell you he's not the talkative type, that lad. In fact, quite the opposite. Polite, yes, no-one can say otherwise. But you never get more than the typical pleasantries from him – "good morning", "good evening" - phrases like that, if you get what I mean.'

'In that case, where did you get the information about the boat and the rest?'

'A fishing friend of mine is the one who told me about him. He moors his boat next to Gassiat's.'

'What's this friend called?'

'Étienne. Étienne Clavé. But don't bother looking for him, because he's not in Arcachon. His second wife is Portuguese, and they always go to her family's house in September.'

'And the name of the boat?'

'The *Elisa*. According to him it comes from an affair he had when he was younger. but he never wanted to tell me anything more. Probably so as not to make his second wife mad.'

'It's the name of Gassiat's boat that we're interested in.'

'The *Hirondelle*. It's a small Estéou from the eighties. but it's still going strong. Although yesterday was a bad day to be on the water. The truth is those boats are much better than the ones they make nowadays. And that lad really looks after his boat. I mean, he doesn't use it for fishing, you can tell, only for those strange trips at night.'

'Why strange?'

'Because he doesn't go out fishing, like I told you. And let's say you don't get much view of the scenery at night.'

'Does he always go out in the boat at night?'

'Recently, yes. Although yesterday the weather was too bad to go sailing. But those little boats are really sturdy. He won't be long getting back. Can you not tell me why you're looking for him?'

'Thank you for your help.'

*

The beach at Aiguillon was deserted. It was too early for tourists or the usual swimmers; besides, it looked like the weather was going to be quite fresh for September, almost like winter. Only a few gulls landed now and again on the sand, casting a quick, unimpressed glance around, then taking off again with empty beaks.

'Not like us, we're about to catch a tasty morsel,' Inspector Canonne said to himself.

The boat they were waiting for came into view.

'There it is,' said detective Masseé who was keeping watch over the entrance to the port through binoculars. 'It fits the description. Look, Inspector!'

Without a doubt it was the one. While they'd waited, they'd checked the model spec. In any case, it was very close now and it was also possible to make out the only person on board, standing at the helm. They detained him as soon as he stepped on the dock. He was wearing warm clothing, typical for being at sea, and a wool cap. Yet what captured their attention most about him, and which Frier would later comment on, was how attractive and elegant he was, naturally elegant, youthful, and at the same time old fashioned. Like a black and white photo. One of those by Robert Doisneau with the handsome young men.

He reacted to the police and their request to go with them to the police station without any surprise, 'as if he were expecting us,' thought Canonne. With a calmness and without any expression of emotion, that you rarely see in the innocent, who are usually quite bewildered. Those who are innocent are usually much more expressive, pulling faces, making gestures, indignant expressions complaining about how unjust their being taken into custody was.

Émile Gassiat did nothing of the kind. He remained silent, passive but not rattled by the police being there. He didn't object to the officers searching the bag that contained his recording equipment, nor the boat where they didn't find anything of interest, nor later his apartment.

The moment they went into the apartment, Canonne said to himself that they had got their man. The reason being that the place was impeccably tidy, more like the methodically kept home of a cold-blooded serial killer rather than a young man of twenty-six. Books and magazines were perfectly lined up on the shelves. The notebooks, the sheet music and the pens and pencils immaculately organised on the desk, the few fine pieces of furniture there were placed as if in a home décor magazine. There was also a grand piano situated in the brightest corner of the room that was used as a living room, dining room and study.

The police found that the bathroom and bedroom were equally as neat and tidy as the main room. In the wardrobe and drawers, they found clothing and fashion accessories all in fine condition and clearly of high quality.

The detectives took photographs. They also took Gassiat's recordings, the computer and the music notebooks for analysis. They stopped at the police station in Arcachon to complete the transfer formalities, and then they put the suspect in the police car to take him to the premises of the Bayonne serious crime squad.

During the journey to Bayonne that lasted for more than two hours, Gassiat remained quietly composed. And he remained the same at the station even when he was being processed into custody. But when he finally went into the room where he would be questioned, standing in front of the empty table he suddenly burst into tears. Silently, without any sign of emotion on his face, tears streamed down his face and fell thick and slow into the man's navy-blue sweater, like drops of acid, thought the Inspector. But teardrops don't burn the skin.

Canonne offered him a box of tissues.

'Sit down, Mr Gassiat. And calm down.'

'Thank you. And forgive me. Hearing about Elisabeth's... Madame Audriard's death has been quite a shock.'

'Since we will be recording, you have the right to have a lawyer present from this moment on.'

'I don't need a lawyer. I've done nothing wrong.'

'As you wish. I'm going to start by asking you about your

relationship with the victim. We know that you were often in contact on the phone.'

'We were friends.'

'Good friends?'

'I don't know what the word "good" might mean for you?'

'Let me rephrase the question for you, were you on intimate terms?'

He didn't answer straightaway. His way of speaking reflected the same care and attention to detail he took in furnishing his home and presumably in the way he had carried out the murder. Immediately, Cannone saw it all so clearly and he took it as a good sign. From experience he knew that murderers frequently fell foul of their own preciseness.

The young man first asked if he could take another tissue.

'As many as you like.'

He wiped his eyes once more and then replied.

'Yes.'

'So "intimate" friends, yes?'

'Yes.'

'Physically intimate?'

'Yes.'

'Does this mean that you had sexual relations with that very old woman?'

'Each to their own.'

'Especially when the women in question are rich.'

He didn't react to the insinuation in Canonne's comment, he simply responded in the same measured tone.

'The money has got nothing to do with it.'

'Answer the question. Were you having a sexual relationship with the victim?'

'Yes.'

He had taken another tissue, he'd wiped his eyes again, but he had moved it away from his face before replying. 'He's replying 'with his face uncovered,' thought Canonne, 'and with the calmness of someone referring to something completely natural.' The Inspector also took this attitude as a good omen. 'He doesn't create spaces in which to hide; he'll end up revealing everything.'

'OK, Mr Gassiat, so you were lovers. And weren't you with her in Biarritz on the day she was murdered? Or in the days previously?'

'No. We hadn't seen each other since June.'

'Did you meet often?'

'Twice a month.'

'In Biarritz?'

'No, always in Paris.'

'In what kind of place did you meet?'

'Cafés, restaurants...'

'Hotels, apartments?'

'Yes, as well.'

'Did you make the reservations?'

'No, she always took care of that.'

'So, you booked into short-stay hotels or apartments?'

'Yes.'

'In other words, just like the apartment in Biarritz where she was murdered and which she had rented despite staying in a fantastic hotel. Weren't you with her that night?'

'I've already told you I hadn't seen her since June.'

'For what reason then would Madame Audiard rent that apartment if it weren't to meet up with you as usual?'

'I don't know. And as I've also told you, we always met in Paris.'

'But now it's summer and people are travelling.'

'We haven't seen each other since June.'

'You are a very young man, and she was an old woman. And also a millionaire. So, it won't surprise you if I ask you if you received some kind of compensation for having a sexual relationship with the victim.'

'What do you mean by compensation?'

'Reward, benefit ... Did you get anything like that for sleeping with the victim?'

'Yes, of course.'

'In what form? Money?'

'No.'

The Inspector thought that Gassiat responded in the way that he must have poured out the acid, slowly, drop by drop. With an exasperating carefulness.

'So what kind of compensation? I need you to be more precise.'

'The satisfaction that lovers hope and search for. All lovers, I suppose.'

'And that would be?'

'Pleasure.'

Canonne felt a stabbing pain in his gum that made everything hurt. He hadn't wanted to bring Laure into the interrogation room, but he had just done so. His head had filled with images of pleasure. Laure's face before, during and after pleasure. And he couldn't help thinking about his wife's last visit. Could he still call her that? A rendezvous that had nothing to do with pleasure due to the damned unsuccessful implant.

'Mr Gassiat, Madame Audiard was eighty years old.'

'Yes, I know.'

'And you are a twenty-six-year-old handsome man. Would you want us to believe that what you sought in this woman was pleasure?'

'Yes. Pleasure. For both of us.' It was said in the most natural way possible, without the slightest hint of shame or doubt.

For Canonne there had never been any doubt that the pleasure he had known with Laure had also been mutual. "For both of us". But now he was missing a tooth and it was like having a key piece missing to all the puzzles of his life that he thought he had completed. Suddenly, he saw a gaping black hole at the centre of so much that he had been certain about. At the centre of the most important aspects. Because at that moment he was thinking about "pleasure for both of us", as if it were something that could be doubted. This questioning was exhausting, he felt that he couldn't carry on, and so he was relieved to see Deputy Inspector Frier gesticulate from behind the glass door for him to come out.

'I'll let you rest for a moment,' he said to the young man. 'And my colleagues will give you something to eat and drink should you wish.'

'Thank you, but I'm fine.'

'We're going to halt the interview anyway. You need to rest a bit.'

'Can I make a phone call?'

'Yes, I've already told you that you have the right to one.'

'I'd like to make it now.'

'Of course. One of my colleagues will assist you.'

'Thank you.'

'Thank goodness that you got me out of there, Frier, I couldn't keep going. The guy has said that he didn't sleep in the boat, that he was awake all night recording the sea, but he doesn't look the slightest bit tired. Whereas I'm beat.'

'I've got something that will cheer you up.' And she took him out to the annex where the technicians were analysing the materials taken from Émile Gassiat's home. 'You have to see this.'

The computer screen displayed curved shapes and artistic flourishes, and although not of the same pattern, they were rather similar to the lines that covered the old woman's body.

'There are loads of files filled with these drawings on Gassiat's computer. And also in the musical notebooks. Look. On many of the pages, along with musical notations on classical sheet music, there are the same type of curved lines, that traced on the paper the gently undulating outline of a landscape, of hills.'

'Or a woman's body', declared Chief Inspector Cannone to himself. And once more he had a vision of Laure.

'Has this cheered you up or not?'

'Of course it has. It seems clearer by the minute that we've got our man. I need you to print out for me one of these files,

Frier. When you have it, please bring it to the interview room along with the photos of the deceased. Faced with this, I don't think it will take him long to confess. It's clear that he is the calculating, methodical kind, but I don't think he's cold-hearted. A moment ago, he started crying.'

'I'm sure he must have a weak spot somewhere.'

'We just have to find it... and these images are going to help us a lot. We need to find that weakness, exploit it and Gassiat will open up like...', the Inspector couldn't find a suitable comparison.

'Like an elevator', Frier finally said, reminded of the title of an old film – Elevator to the Gallows – or at least confession and prison.

'For a long stretch.'

'Yes. By the way, have you already checked his mobile?'

'No activity since June. It's quite a recent model with a geolocation app. And what data history tells us is that it hasn't left his apartment in Arcachon all summer.'

'It doesn't matter. Everyone knows that carrying a mobile gives away your whereabouts and your movements. He could have left it in apartment on purpose, as an alibi, before travelling to Biarritz.'

'We already know that on 27th August the calls made to the victim were made from an old mobile phone with a different number.'

'Which the killer could easily have got rid of later. What's important are these drawings and the image of the dead woman. Get them ready and bring them to me.'

Inspector Canonne returned to the interview room. It looked as if the suspect hadn't moved from where he was sitting.

'Have you made your phone call?'

'Yes, thank you.' His attitude certainly hadn't changed. He remained just as calm as he had been earlier, perhaps even calmer, because his eyes now were perfectly dry, without the slightest sign of having shed tears.

'Where were you the day that Madame Audiard was killed?'

'In Arcachon. I've hardly moved from there all summer.'

'Explain to me what you mean by "hardly".'

'I've only been out on the water a few days.'

'Nights, you mean.'

'Yes, nights.'

'Why is it at night that you go out to sea?'

'Because there's no-one else out on the water, and also the noises coming from the surroundings are stilled.'

'And you've done nothing else?'

'I've also gone to Bordeaux a few times.'

'For any specific reason?'

He seemed to hesitate.

'To go for a wander or go shopping,' he said finally.

'I see. You're a spender, aren't you? You enjoy buying things.'

'No, not at all.'

'And yet, in your apartment we saw quite a range of clothing and accessories, and not exactly of the cheap kind. How do you make a living, Mr Gassiat? Do you work?'

'I'm a composer.' Inspector Canonne remembered the pathologist's recommendation – 'look for someone with artistic tendencies.'

'And you can earn a living from that?'

'Not at the moment, but I hope to one day.'

'And in the meantime, how do you eat and look after your boat, and travel to Paris, and buy expensive clothes?'

'My parents died some years ago. They left me a small inheritance and I also received compensation, because they were killed in a car accident. With that money I can keep going a while longer, without any kind of income.'

'How much is the grand piano worth that we saw in your house? According to the notes given to me by a colleague... a Yamaha...'. Deputy Inspector Frier came in at that moment and put down a file on the desk between them.

'Thanks, Frier.'

Émile Gassiat waited for the officer to leave before replying:

'Yes, a Yamaha C5X. You can put it in silent mode and play without annoying the neighbours.'

'How much is it worth?'

'About €40,000.'

'Did you pay for it yourself?'

'No, it was a present.'

'From the victim?

'No.'

'I'm going to ask you again because I'm not altogether sure about this. Did you receive money from the murdered old woman or any other women?'

'No.'

'But presents, yes?'

'Sometimes, yes.'

'Presents as expensive as a piano worth €40,000?'

'The value of a gift is not measured by the price. It's all relative.'

'Don't give me that cheap philosophical nonsense. And anyway, you only seem interested in what's expensive.'

The Inspector waited for a reaction from Gassiat, for his attitude to crack in some way. To no avail. The suspect didn't respond, didn't make the slightest gesture. So Canonne opened the file, slowly placing photos from the scene of the crime in front of the young man one by one.

'I want you to look carefully at these photos. We took them of madame Audiard, your intimate friend, when we found her murdered in a flat in Biarritz that was not of the highest standing, although the cost of everything is relative.'

Gassiat looked slowly at the photos placed before him by the inspector. Whatever impact they had on him, he kept his feelings to himself. The inspector grew impatient again.

'Well, enough of the rhetoric! Did you kill her?'

'No.'

'Did you make these drawings on her skin?'

'No.'

'Why do they seem so much like the drawings found in your notebooks and computer?' he asked, handing Gassiat the page that had been printed out by Frier.

'These are in no way similar.'

'I am inclined to disagree. I can see the same hand and the same purpose at work here.'

'What you can see on this page are the sound waves of the sea. I record them and then I make these drawings... and from this I imagine new musical lines.'

'Mr Gassiat, did you murder her? And once she was dead, did you draw these macabre musical lines on her skin?'

The young man covered his face with his hands. His fingers were long and slim, like a woman's, thought the Inspector. Hands familiar with slow, meticulous, delicate gestures. Drop by drop.

'Did you kill her?'

'No. Please stop with this. No. No. I would never harm her, even in the slightest way.'

'And yet, you used a false name with her: Maurice Darbo. Do you recognise it?'

'You already know about that.'

'We do, yes,' the Inspector responded without giving any more details; he didn't want to mention the second woman. 'Do you acknowledge you know this name?'

'Yes, but it isn't a false name, it's my professional name. It's the one I use for my compositions.'

'Is your real name not good enough?'

'It's hard to explain, but I wanted a fresh start with the music.'

'And you need a different name for that?'

'Yes.'

'An artistic name, let's say.'

'Yes, you could put it like that.' And Canonne thought that, in the end, the young pathologist wasn't far off the mark.

At dusk he called the coroner, who wanted to see the Inspector straight away. Canonne liked working with Coroner

Maillard, because he was passionate about his work and went deep into every case, never leaving any loose ends or letting any clue go un-investigated, no matter however improbable or crazy it seemed at first. He also maintained a very cordial and seamless relation with the police based on trust and respect, as he often repeated to the Inspector in a warm and friendly tone. But on this occasion Maillard received him quite coldly, in an almost offhand manner:

'Any results, Inspector?'

'For the moment, no, your Honour. But I'm convinced we've got our man. He's already admitted that he was the old woman's lover.'

'And that she paid him?'

'No, he didn't want to admit to that. He says that she gave him gifts. But it fits with the psychological profile that the pathologist gave us, and he doesn't have an alibi for either the day or the night of the murder. And we have something quite important, I would even say crucial.'

'What is it?'

'We found something at his home, on his computer and in his notebooks, some line drawings that even though they aren't identical, they are reminiscent of those the murderer traced on the victim's skin.'

'Have you brought them with you so I can see them?'

'Yes.'

Canonne offered him the file that contained various sheets of paper covered with these lines and photographs of the body. The judge looked at them carefully for quite a while.

'Inspector, do you really think they look similar?' he asked at last. 'I'm not so sure.'

'Not exactly, but they're close. And Gassiat seems quite careful, not at all the type of person who would make the mistake of keeping identical designs in his house.'

'And yet he has kept these.'

'Maybe out of interest; his explanation is that these repeated pattens echo the melodic lines found in his compositions.'

31

'I see, I don't have to remind you, Canonne, how delicate this matter is. The woman who was murdered had powerful friends everywhere. We need to close this case as soon as possible.'

'Above all because there's a second woman in Paris.'

'Yes, they told me. None other than Irène Duroudier.'

'We've spoken with her over the phone, but she was unable to give us anything that was really of any use. She only knew the victim incidentally and had no idea she had anything to do with Gassiat. Actually, to her he wasn't Émile Gassiat, but Maurice Darbo. An artistic name, as he puts it.'

'Did he use a false name with the dead woman?'

'Yes, he's admitted that, even though we didn't tell him how we obtained that information. We haven't spoken to him yet about the second woman.'

'Do you know which family that woman belongs to?' Canonne used the exact same words the prosecutor had chosen to describe the victim when they opened the case.

'To a highly prominent family, with influential friends in very high places.'

'Right. And even worse, if you catch my drift. I've just been informed that she's the aunt of someone high up in the government. Very high up.'

'Gassiat has requested his phone call and she's the person he called. To the same mobile we had logged.'

'That's all we need. He must have had a very good relationship with her. How long has he been detained?'

'Since 8.45 this morning.'

'Ok, so bring him here at the same time tomorrow. I want to start questioning him myself as soon as possible. And we'll wait here until the lawyer he's hired from Paris arrives. Someone's in quite a hurry in the capital.'

That lawyer was called Albert Larten. Judge Maillard didn't know him, but he had searched his profile on the internet. Another eccentric in sexual matters, he thought on seeing Larten's photos online. Just what wasn't needed for a case like this that had appeared on his desk. Because it was certain that anyone with the physical characteristics that this lawyer had was going to call attention to themselves, and all the more so in the court room, in the city, in the media.

'Mr Larten, do you know him, Inspector?

'I came up against him...' Canonne was about to reply, but he stopped himself. 'We were on the same case some years ago.'

'Quite a character, from what I've seen on the internet.'

'Yes, indeed. I thought he wasn't practising law anymore and was now a private detective.'

'And wine critic.'

3

The Others

Larten helped the old woman into the campervan. The inside was sparse but comfortable. Two antique-blue leather armchairs, placed on either side of a folding table made of beech. In the same pale wood, well-finished cupboards and several shelves filled with perfectly aligned legal documents, novels and wine guides.

Larten offered the woman the chair nearest the door, the one he reserved for clients.

'I have to say, it's quite original', said the woman sitting down and placing her bag on the table, 'I can't think there are many lawyers in Paris who will have set up their office in a campervan.'

'The truth is I work mainly as a private investigator, as I already told you over the phone, and you should have seen this on my web page.'

'All the better. I think we're going to need both of your professions for this matter. And in any case, I don't think there are many detectives with an office like yours either, Mr Larten. If I may call you so.'

'Larten will do just fine.'

'I imagine it's practical. I mean the mobile office.'

'Yes, this job means having to travel quite a lot.'

'And you prefer to have everything close to hand at all times.'

'I suppose you're right.'

She had rested her hands on the table, and they were trembling. But even though this woman had already turned eighty, it wasn't age that made her fingers shake so violently. Not violent, no; Larten immediately banished that word from his mind. You could sense a great strength in that woman but without any trace of violence. The trembling of her hands was produced by a powerful emotion that Larten could not yet identify.

'First of all, I'd like to thank you, Larten, for receiving me so promptly. I've already explained to you on the phone, in broad terms, what the situation is and the urgency as well. But what I haven't told you yet is why I've chosen you. And I'd like, if it's OK with you, to tell you now. I think it can influence your decision whether to accept the case or not to my satisfaction.'

'I'm listening.'

'My family is, among other pursuits, involved in the wine business and is therefore familiar with your website. I'm going to spare you the unpleasant comments they once made about you, when I was with them.'

Larten smiled. He was beginning to like this woman.

'But I want you to know that if there is anything that they don't like, the same doesn't apply to me. What they find reprehensible, let's leave it at that term, about your appearance and your demeanour, I find interesting and stimulating. So, I dug into your profile a bit and followed your *The Wine Detective* blog posts regularly. Not knowing, of course, that one day I would have need of you. But that day has come. Because not only do I want a lawyer to get that young man out of police custody as soon as possible, but also a detective capable of finding the real culprit so that the suspicions and misunderstandings end once and for all. I also want someone who looks at him and his life choices, obviously with respect, but also naturally, that is, without being surprised. What is accepted as natural stops surprising us. And I think that you, Larten, are the best person to understand what I am proposing here, because you'll surely have wanted that kind of openness for yourself as well.'

'Thank you for your trust.'

'That's why I've come to ask you to represent him.'

Perhaps the emotion that made not only her hands tremble but now also her chin and her lips was the embarrassment of having to ask: 'I need you, I ask you, I come to ask you...', for someone who was used only to giving orders. She must have cared a great deal about that young man. Larten turned in his chair to get a pen and a notebook from one of the cupboards.

'Does that mean you'll take on the case?'

'Let me get a more precise idea of the situation first. You seem very sure of that young man's innocence, was he with you the day of the crime? Can you provide some kind of alibi for him?'

'If he had been with me, I would've told the police immediately. Don't think I would've hesitated for an instant. But he wasn't with me. We don't see each other in summer, they are very difficult months, everyone insists on getting together. But Maurice is incapable... well, actually his name is not Maurice but Émile, the police told me, Émile Gassiat.'

'It doesn't help that he's been using a fake name.'

'Do you really think this is important?'

'It's not what's important to me, Madame Duroudier.'

'Irène, please.'

'Rather how this hurts his credibility.'

'Maurice or Émile, it doesn't matter, he's incapable of doing such a thing and he's also assured me over the phone that he's innocent and I believe him. And anyway, what does a false name mean? Which one is the real one? The one we didn't choose and yet haunts us in every document, bank card, plane ticket, medical record, hotel room? Is the name true even though the life isn't true or even truly a life? Some names are a heavy burden and a hindrance to happiness. I understand if someone wants to choose their own.'

'How long have you known him?'

'A little over three years.'

'Did you see each other regularly?'

'Two or three times a month. And we wrote to each other from time to time. Letters the old-fashioned way, on paper.'

'Have you kept them?'

'No. And I'm sure he hasn't either. We agreed to destroy them once we'd read them.'

'Why? You just told me you trusted him.'

'Him, yes, Larten, obviously; but we are not alone in the world.'

'Did you know the victim, Elisabeth Audiard?'

'I knew who she was, of course. In some circles you always end up coming across the same names and references to the same people. But I had no relationship with that woman.'

'And that she was seeing Émile, did you know about that?'

'No. Maurice... I prefer to keep calling him that, by his chosen name. Maurice doesn't share every aspect of his life with me, and I do the same. Let's say we have our common space and then there's the rest.'

'You already told me over the phone that this woman was found dead in a rented apartment. Did you also meet Émile in such places or hotels?'

'No. Always in an apartment on the rue Claude Bernard that I own privately and not to the knowledge of others. I mean, outside the current properties and inventory of family assets. I've managed to keep the apartment separate from everything and everyone.'

'Who has a key to that apartment?'

'Only me.'

'Have you never given or lent it to Émile?'

'It's not been necessary. He usually arrives by train from Bordeaux, takes a taxi or the metro and I wait for him at home.'

'Does someone take care of the cleaning?'

'Yes. But I deal with that woman myself.'

'So nobody can enter the flat without you?'

'Unless they pick the lock, which has never happened. You can imagine how important it is for me to preserve the privacy of that space.'

'It's precisely that privacy that I'd need us to talk about now. Can I offer you something to drink?'

'Yes, maybe some water, thanks.'

Larten got up, took two glasses from one of the cupboards, and a bottle of mineral water from a small refrigerator, the door of which was panelled in the same pale wood. He poured it into the two glasses and sat down again in front of his client. Because she was going to be his client; he had already decided.

'I need to ask you about the intimacy you shared with Émile; and my questions may make you uncomfortable.'

'Don't worry. You won't have to ask them. I know what you need to know, and I am going to answer you candidly.'

Before starting, she took a sip of water.

'Maurice and I are lovers. I'm not going to deny that, in my already long life, I've sometimes lost my head; but what I've never lost is the sense of the ridiculous. So, the sexual relations we have aren't financially motivated, as I believe it's called nowadays. Anyway, I don't pay the young man to sleep with me. I'm rich, and so I make his life easier or more pleasant sometimes, with a gift. But we are not linked by money. And, by the way, seeing as I'm in this van with you, what type's yours?'

'Are you referring to me or the campervan?' Larten smiled. As did she, for the first time.

'I already have a good idea,' responded Irène Duroudier, still smiling, 'I mean about the campervan.'

'It's a Mercedes Sprinter.'

'I like it. So, to what I was saying a moment ago. Maurice and I are not tied together by money. And if I'm in this Sprinter with you, it's because I think you're going to accept the true nature of our relationship, and simply take it as it is.'

'Without being shocked.'

'Not in the slightest.'

'Exactly. That's how I consider it. And I agree to take the case.'

Larten had had a hard time understanding the emotion coursing through his client's body, but he finally understood. It wasn't embarrassment but pride. The pride of still feeling that desire in her, at her age. And the pride that this desire was reciprocated.

Irène Duroudier opened her bag and took out a bulky yellow envelope. She set it down on the table and gently pushed it toward Larten.

'Inside you will find the notes that I've taken from what the police and Maurice himself explained to me when he called me from the police station. I've also added some details about us: dates, gifts, some information, let's say practical, that I imagine will be useful in an investigation like the one you're about to start, and that I prefer to let you have in writing. You'll also find some money for your first expenses. We don't need to discuss your fees. I will accept whatever you decide. What I ask is that you go and help him as soon as possible. He's been detained in Bayonne.'

'I'll catch the first flight to Biarritz tomorrow morning.'

'Thank you. Then I await your news.'

And with that she got up. Larten did the same.

'Do you want me to drop you somewhere?'

'I appreciate the offer, but it's not necessary. My driver is waiting for me not far from here.'

He helped her down and watched her walk away, slowly, hesitating slightly, yet with no sign of weakness or feeling in danger.

And he saw himself, many years ago, when he was still a child, one afternoon after leaving school. He had begun to walk towards his house, dazed, as if dizzy, by the discoveries he had just made; and yet he advanced with a firm and determined step, and without lowering his head, because deep inside he felt happy and proud of himself.

Irène Duroudier got into the car; the chauffeur closed the door behind her, got back behind the wheel; and the sumptuous blue Bentley came around the corner, turned left, and was gone.

At school, that afternoon, they had begun to analyse *Father Goriot*, which was going to be the set text for the whole term. In that book Balzac had imagined the Vauquer house: a "bourgeois pension for both sexes and others". And he, a child just like any other, a child still indistinguishable from the others, reading that curious description in his book, had understood, with the incredible intuition of childhood, two things that were going to be fundamental in his life, and that, on the way home, produced in him an emotion that made him tremble but, at the same time, kept him on his feet, like Irène Duroudier.

The first told him that later, when he'd grown up and the time came, he would belong to the category of "others". The second, that great novels are always to be trusted and that he was going to become a devoted, grateful reader.

*

Albert Larten was forty-five years old, but everyone told him he looked much younger. Perhaps because in his dark hair, which he always kept very short, there was not even the slightest trace of grey. He was tall, close to six feet tall, broad-shouldered, and with a tendency to gain pounds that he managed to keep at bay by keeping a close eye on his diet and taking long walks. Walking was one of his passions and Paris was probably the best setting in the world to indulge it.

When he wasn't travelling, he tried to walk everywhere. When he went anywhere in his campervan, he parked far enough from his destination to be able to walk a good distance there and back. This time he would travel by plane, he had to get to Bayonne as soon as possible. But once there, he would find the time to walk through that area that he was very familiar with, and which had for him, among other attractions, its vineyards: the terraces of Irouléguy... the hills where the light and lively txakoli grapes look out over the sea, on the other side of the border.

Besides, walking helped him think; not only to organise the ideas that had already formed in his head, but also to open spaces, clear paths, so the new could surface and circulate freely. To walk was a means to encourage the imagination.

He'd just read the notes that Irène Duroudier had handed to him, and it certainly couldn't be claimed that the investigators had given much thought to the case. For them, the fact that a twenty-six-year-old man sleeps with an eighty-year-old woman, who is also rich, follows a single pattern, which of course has an unambiguous name. And whoever easily thinks "kept man" or "gigolo", can also think just as easily of the things that make said young man, in an instant, the number one suspect.

Larten liked cars a lot, but he had never been attracted to automatic transmissions. He preferred to decide for himself when to switch from one gear to another. It was the same with people; he didn't appreciate the "automatic" mind sets, going from one thought to another, pushed, not by their own reflection, but by the mechanism, always set, always ready to intervene, based on prior judgement and prejudice.

He finished dressing. For his date with Monique, he had chosen the cobalt blue suit that she particularly liked, and that he could wear the next day to his client's appearance before the coroner. His idea was to sleep at his girlfriend's house and leave from there for the airport early the next morning.

He packed several shirts and ties, a more casual pair of trousers and a sweater; pyjamas, two silk scarves, his toiletry bag; and a trench coat, because the weather in the Basque Country was turning autumnal. He closed the suitcase and took it to the hallway.

He'd arranged to meet Monique at half past eight. He had plenty of time to finish getting ready and walk to her house.

If he hadn't had that court appearance in Bayonne the next day, he would have painted his nails with the urban grey nail polish he'd just bought. But removing the nail polish before getting to Bayonne was going to be a pain and appearing in front of the judge with painted nails would be ramping it up too much. He'd choose something more discreet for this occasion. Something with just a 'hint' that would allow him to play his part in such a serious matter, without ceasing to be himself.

Just as a small question mark can alter the course and meaning of an entire sentence, no matter how complex and articulate it might be, Larten wanted those feminine touches that he included in his appearance or in his clothing, to act as a question mark at the end of each of the "sentences" that constituted his identity. Something that would trouble others, getting them to question their own identity or fall for his charms. An invitation to dive into the unknown.

He put on high-heeled boots. And he smiled, telling himself that it was lucky that young women were wearing them so high at the moment. For dinner he also wore lipstick. He took the suitcase and went out towards the Rue du Pré-aux-Clercs. He would go down the streets slowly to the Quai Malaquais; and would cross the Seine by the Pont des Arts.

Monique lived across the river, on the Rue de Lancy. It was barely a quarter past seven. He could take a nice walk and get to her house on time. At the Pont des Arts he could hear the wind whistling like a man. Like someone who wants to attract attention, Larten thought, to be heard. He stopped and walked over to the railing. The Seine flowed calmly but resolutely towards its unalterable destiny: to the wide of the mouth of the river first and then on to the vastness of the open sea. Paris witnessed how that journey to freedom unfolded before her eyes at every moment... Without pause, without hesitation, without fear, the river advanced towards that freedom, day after day, year after year, century after century, reaffirming and transmitting its message of independence and openness with its magnificent persuasive beauty. And Larten thought that was exactly what the wind wanted to bring to mind with the provocation of its voice.

If it couldn't be accepted in Paris that an older person could arouse desire in a much younger one, then where? Or that a man could desire a woman in two ways, as he did, blending his manly desire with the desire that one woman feels for another, then where?

Larten turned away from the railing, crossed the bridge and continued on his way with the image of the Seine in his mind. Its serene but unwavering course. Its constant transfer of women and men and "others" as in Balzac's novel. If that diversity was not understood, respected, or welcomed in Paris, then where else in the world?

He tapped in the access code and entered Monique's doorway. In front of the elevator mirror, he touched up the lipstick on his lips. He knocked on the door. Monique opened it with a smile. She had put on a tight, low-cut black dress, which he loved. But as soon as she saw him, the smile faded from her face:

'If you know that I dislike you wearing makeup, why do you do it? And even more so when I invite you to my house for dinner.'

'Good evening, my darling. I hope you're going to invite me in for something more. I've brought my suitcase. I'd like to leave here early tomorrow for the airport.'

Monique stepped back from the door to let him in.

'And to top it off, those heels that make you look like a giant. So that everything is more visible and more offensive.'

'You know it's not meant to be offensive, Monique, but rather to be honest with myself; and with you.'

'I'm sorry Albert, but I just can't get used to it.'

'Well, let me help you.'

But she wouldn't let him. She didn't want to let him. Monique experienced that peculiarity of her lover as if she were on a wire suspended in the air, always about to fall to one side, that of complete rejection; or to the other, of fully accepting Larten, which also meant accepting her own fusion of desires. But she didn't fall, she managed to keep her balance over the conflict caused by his nails or lipstick or heels or jewellery or the fantasy of Larten's underwear; about the confusion that all these elements brought, beyond mere appearance, into their own intimacy. But she didn't fall.

She fought against Larten's sexual eccentricity but didn't completely exclude it. She let it be part of their relationship. And Larten admired her and loved her more for it. It's easy to stick with what doesn't bother you. It's easy to settle into what doesn't challenge or disturb. Monique had agreed to live with him through the difficult times, on what she sometimes called "rough terrain", when she was in a good mood.

'So, what do I do Monique, do I stay or go back home?'

'You're staying.'

And she took him by the waist and pulled him towards her.

'You must take off those boots if you want me to kiss you on the lips. If not, I'll never reach.'

*

Émile Gassiat had confirmed the statements he had made at the police station before the judge.

'However,' said Judge Maillard, 'I would like to return to some points, to give you the opportunity to clarify your answers or to rectify any if you wish. It is still not too late.'

'Everything is correct.'

'So, you insist on affirming that apart from the victim, Elisabeth Audiard and Irène Duroudier with whom we have already spoken... that apart from those two ladies, you have no other lady friends with whom you're intimate?'

And he had pronounced the word "intimate" with such blatant disgust that Larten immediately understood two things. The first, that what the judge was most interested in was finding out if there were more women from high society involved in the matter, that is, determining the magnitude of the scandal that the Biarritz murder could cause, and the pressure that this was going to put on his work. On the one hand, the press had to be kept away from the kind of news a case like this would generate. This was not going to be easy at all. On the other hand, he had to avoid falling like a fly into the web that was going to be woven, which was undoubtedly already being woven, around the murder of Elisabeth Audiard; a tight mesh of influences, recommendations, an urgency to resolve the matter as soon and as satisfactorily as possible. 'Maillard sees himself as an insect that is about to fall into that sticky web,' thought Larten, 'and he is not going to take the slightest risk.'

The second thing he understood was that the judge was going to order the preventive detention of Émile Gassiat, despite the weakness of case against him, because he was not going to risk seeing the naked corpse, covered with horrible burns, of another eminent woman appear on a third-rate bed. And that for this reason the rest of the interrogation, as if under the effect of a magnifying glass, was going to be solely aimed at increasing the probability that the detainee, who answered the questions with a disconcerting calmness, was indeed the cold, meticulous killer the forensic report described.

'And he's also a gigolo,' Larten reckoned the judge was thinking.

'So, no one can confirm what you did on August 28th last. Neither on the 27th, nor for that matter on the 29th.'

'I went on the water alone, at night, to record the sounds of the sea.'

'The files of the recorder usually record the exact dates and times in which the recordings were made,' Larten indicated, 'It is easy to verify.'

'We'll check it, Mr Larten, don't worry. But I imagine that the data in those files can be altered at will, is that not so, Mr. Gassiat?'

'I guess so,' Émile answered, 'but that's not what I do. I

need to keep the exact date, time and place of each sound.'

'So, on the night of August 28th, the night of the crime, you were at sea. Where?'

'Near Arcachon, not far from the coast. It's a small boat.'

'But you could have sailed to Biarritz, anchored there, and later made the return trip. Is it possible, isn't it?'

'I don't know. I have never made such a long trip with my boat. I only go out on the water at night, without going too far from the coast, as I have told you; just for a few hours, and then I come home.'

'Is that what you did the night of August 27th, and the 29th as well?'

'Yes.'

'But nobody can confirm this.'

'That's what I've been told. I didn't talk to anyone.'

'And during the day, after returning from sea, what did you do?'

'What I usually do. Rest a bit and compose my music, from the sounds of the sea that I have recorded.'

'Yes, and which you then turn into those melodic lines that are so reminiscent of the marks by made the murderer on Madame Audiard's body. You've seen them too.'

' Yes, they've shown me the photographs.'

'Don't you think that those marks are very reminiscent of the traces of the drawings that we found in your house?'

'No. I don't see any resemblance.'

It's not going to help us either, Larten thought, if Gassiat keeps speaking in this monotonous tone, without hesitation or any sign of emotion. If a defendant seemed composed, it was very often viewed with suspicion. It was interpreted, from the outset, in a negative way; to view them not as having a clear conscience, but as having a cold and calculating manipulative personality, as someone accustomed to deception.

'I'm going to show you those pictures again.'

The judge handed the young man the closed folder. Émile rested it on his knees, opened it and began to go through the photographs slowly, without altering his calm expression, not even when faced with those horrible images. Larten was sure he was acting this way not out of coldness or indifference, but out of an extreme form of embarrassment. He wished he could tell him at that moment to stop it, to let everything go; but that would only have aggravated his client's situation. It wasn't going to be the tactic of letting his emotions show, as suggested by a lawyer, that was going to positively influence the judge, quite the opposite.

'What do you feel when you see these images of Elisabeth Audiard dead and having been attacked in such a horrible way with acid?'

Émile Gassiat closed the folder and, as if he didn't know what to do with it, turned to Larten, who took it and handed it back to the judge.

'I feel pain.'

But it was a pain the young man foolishly held inside; a feeling that was heard but not seen; and that wasn't going to help him.

'What kind of pain, can you be more precise?'

'The one you feel for the disappearance of someone you care about. And also, the pain of imagining what they must have suffered in the end, before they died.'

The judge shifted his position in the chair and also his gaze on Gassiat. He is looking at him now, thought Larten, like a runner, who is far ahead of the rest of the field, looks toward the finishing line, knowing that he is already very close to his goal and no one can rob him of victory.

'So have you thought about that kind of ending?'

'Yes.'

'And what do you think it's like?'

'I'm told it was acid that made those marks. I guess it hurts terribly when it touches the body.'

'Have you ever handled it?'

'No, but I've already suffered a burn in the kitchen or with the boat's engine and I know how much it hurts, even when the burn is small. So I imagine she must've suffered terribly.'

'She was already dead when they doused her with the acid, didn't you know that?'

'No, but I'm glad about that, because that way she didn't suffer while they burned her.'

The finishing line was much further away than the runner had thought a moment ago. And the judge was beginning to show signs of impatience.

'I guess you know what morphine is,' he said, raising his voice a little.

'Yes.'

'Have you ever used it?'

'No.'

'But you know how it's administered.'

'Yes, I've seen it in documentaries or in movies.'

'You can also search for information on the internet. Have you?'

'No.'

'Is there anyone in your circle of friends who is treated with morphine?'

'Not that I know of.'

'Are you sure? Older people, like the women you see, sometimes suffer from chronic pain that can be very severe.'

'Not that I know of,' Gassiat repeated, in the same imperturbable tone.

The judge wrote something down in his notebook and underlined it with an ostensible double stroke, before continuing the questioning.

'Let's return to the crime. Madame Audiard had been injected with a deadly dose of morphine and then burned by drawing the lines you already know about on her body. Do you insist on claiming it wasn't you?

'He's already done so several times, Your Honour,' Larten then said. 'I think there's no doubt about it.'

'Let your client answer, Mr Larten, and let me decide what is doubtful or not.'

'So, Mr. Gassiat, it was not you who killed and burned Elisabeth Audiard?'

'It wasn't me.'

'Are you sure?'

'Yes. I wouldn't do...' he hesitated a moment but only to correct the tense. 'I wouldn't have done her any harm; never.'

'But no one can confirm that you weren't with her, in that apartment in Biarritz, on August 28th.'

'No one can confirm that he was with her either, Your Honour,' Larten replied.

'I will phrase my question in another way. Can anyone confirm that you were in Arcachon on the night of August 28th?'

'I don't know. I don't think so.'

'Apparently you play the piano very often.'

'Yes, almost every day.'

'And nobody heard you in that building with such thin walls, "like cigarette paper" to use the expression of your neighbour on the landing?'

'I have already told the police that the piano can be put in silent mode. It doesn't produce sound out loud, only I can hear the music with the headphones connected. At home I always play it like this.'

'So no-one saw or heard you. No friend or flatmate of your own age?'

'I'm almost always alone.'

'Except when you are with your elderly "friends".'

'Yes.'

'Do these kinds of relationships seem natural to you, Mr. Gassiat?'

'They're not typical, but I'm not the only one who's interested in older women.'

'Especially if they're rich.'

'Money has nothing to do with it.'

'OK right; I'm going to ask you again, apart from Madame Audiard and Madame Duroudier, who is already aware of what's going on, do you have the same type of relationship with any other older woman?'

'No, I already told you.'

'Yes, and you have also declared that you didn't pay for the very special and expensive piano you have in your house, rather it was given to you.'

'That is correct.'

'Was it the late Madame Audiard who gave you such a generous gift?'

'No.'

'So, who? Madame Duroudier?'

Emile Gassiat turned back to Larten.

'Do I have to answer that question?'

Larten shook his head, giving a discreet warning in a deep voice, like a light that suddenly switches red on a dashboard, silent but saying so much.

'You're not obliged to answer, Émile, but it would be advisable to do so.'

'You don't have to answer anything if you don't want to,' the judge added quickly. 'We have already informed you of your right to remain silent. But everything is important, everything counts. What is said and what is not.'

'Then I prefer to keep silent,' answered the young man.

'As you wish. But everything counts.'

For Larten there was no doubt. That silence of his client resonated like the hammer marking the end of an auction. Preventive detention had been awarded. Because that silence loudly evoked the existence of the other woman, Irène Duroudier, belonging to a family that was also very powerful. And perhaps even, despite the young man's repeated denials, that of other women. There was not the slightest material evidence against Émile Gassiat; but the victim was too important, and this murder, an act capable of putting half of upper-class France, the cream of society, on alert and into action. A cream that, of course, was not going to mobilise to defend the gigolo, but was going to shake his influences, to cushion as much as possible the impact produced by the discovery of the crime and the peculiar sexual life of his victim. The powerful families of the women involved were not going to lift a finger to save that young man, in whom they would see nothing more than a vulgar kept man; because doing so could also be interpreted as a way to legitimise the sexual whims of their "grandmothers". Something Larten considered the judge would find, "absolutely unimaginable."

'I'm going to ask you one last time. Are there other older women you have relationships with?'

'No.'

'Are you sure?'

'Yes.'

He was taken to the old jail in Bayonne, the so-called Villa Chagrin, Villa Grief.

That young man was a lover of old women who in one way or another supported him and with whom he used a false name; he had no alibi for the day or night of the crime. He was the creator of those disturbing drawings, and he also owned a boat that would have allowed him to travel by sea to Biarritz, thus avoiding the security cameras placed on the roads; and then get rid of the acid and the rest of the elements used in the crime by throwing them overboard.

He was already in custody, and everyone seemed satisfied, or at least relieved, by the result of an investigation that had been concluded cleanly, quickly and, in the words of the prosecutor, without excessive "media fanfare", which seemed to be regarded as the most important thing.

'We must avoid an avalanche of implications,' the prosecutor had added, 'just like a real avalanche, Inspector, capable of destroying everything in its path.'

To guarantee that same discretion, the case, which could have been transferred to the Paris prosecutor's office, remained in Bayonne, in preparation for the forthcoming trial before the Court of Assizes in Pau.

'Congratulations, Inspector, you have done a good job,'

Canonne's superior had said to him, 'and naturally I'll keep you at the head of the investigation. We must put together a solid case for the trial. I'm counting on your efficiency.'

But Inspector Canonne could not be happy with the result of his work, not even at peace. Everything had been too fast and especially too easy. An ease and a speed that did not match at all the sophisticated and methodical execution of the crime. There was something there that just didn't quite click. The judge, the prosecutor, and no doubt also the victim's family, were satisfied with the arrest of Émile Gassiat that stifled the scandal, like a blanket thrown over a flame in time, managing to suffocate the start of a potentially devastating fire. But Canonne couldn't find the same satisfaction; his body reacted to the contrary. It was like a titanium implant that couldn't find a place to screw into.

*

Larten had booked a room at the Grand Hotel in Bayonne. From there he could walk to the prison in the Saint Esprit district, on the other side of the Adour. A walk of about twenty minutes each time to get their ideas organised.

Although he didn't have many ideas in this case. As it stood, he had very few solid elements. I only have "fluid" theories, he said to himself as he went down to breakfast in the hotel dining room – purely subjective: Madame Duroudier's confidence in the young man's innocence; and the statement, repeated over and over again, by Gassiat himself that 'I would never have done the slightest harm to Elisabeth.'

To all the above Larten could only add his own intuition, an argument that was not worth much in court but to which he clung. His intuition had failed him on very few occasions in his life, perhaps because he was a good wine taster. And what we call intuition could surely be explained as heightened awareness and alertness of the five senses.

He took the newspapers, sat down at a table at the back of

the dining room, and ordered the special breakfast. Later he would make up for the excess, walking briskly to jail. The press was surprisingly quiet about the case. Just a few lines containing the identification and preventive imprisonment of E.G., the alleged murderer of Biarritz. Of "Biarritz" the newspapers said, without mentioning Elisabeth Audiard. And Larten thought again of the "others", not of those who found a room in the Vauquer de Balzac pension; but of those "others" capable of guiding the course of the press and of the court records and of the necessities of desire... Those "others" who were going to have to be convinced of Gassiat's innocence with arguments infinitely more palpable than intuitions and tender words.

Larten returned to his room, put on a silk scarf around his neck and the same boots from the day before. They were high-heeled and yet very comfortable to walk in. The kind of paradox he loved so much.

They showed Larten to the room where he could speak in private with his client. Émile Gassiat was already waiting for him there, sitting at a small table, his hands resting on the edge, as if on the keyboard of a piano he was about to play.

He was dressed in the clothes he had been given in prison, but he didn't look like a prisoner, or at least, not a prisoner in a true story. He seemed more like an actor involved in a prison drama. An actor who wears the same uniform as everyone else and yet you immediately see that he is different, Larten thought. Not only because it's very possible that you have recognised the actor, but above all because freedom is very difficult to hide, and the actor is a free man. All his gestures and expressions betray this fact, despite the thick layers of makeup and the script guidelines, the confidence he has in his freedom; his certainty that as soon as "cut" is heard and the lights go out, he will be able to get up and leave the false prison on set.

It's exactly what it seems like, Larten thought when seeing, through the glass of the visiting booth, his client who was waiting for him calmly, without showing signs of anxiety or fear – an actor who cannot hide that he is free.

When Larten entered the room, the young man stood up and held out his hand. A courtesy gesture that also belonged to another context, as if they were not in a prison but in an everyday setting, a café or a salon. They sat facing each other.

'It's a very old prison,' was the first thing Larten said to his client.

'Yes, you can see that right away.'

'And I don't know how reliable these walls are for ensuring the confidentiality of what we say to each other. So, to make you feel more comfortable, I invite you to try to speak as quietly as possible.'

'OK.'

'And let's speak without formalities.'

'I prefer to be formal if you don't mind. It comes more naturally to me.'

'Then me too. How are you?'

'I'm fine, don't worry. I have been given a single cell. I just wanted to know how long you think they're going to keep me here.'

'I'm afraid quite a long time if we don't get something convincing that can support your version of events or guide the investigation in another direction. And as it stands, we have nothing. So, I'm going to get straight to the point.'

'OK.'

'There is something that neither the police nor the judge have asked you. It must have seemed unnecessary to them, since you readily acknowledged your relationship with Madame Audiard.'

'Which is?'

'How did you meet her? When, where, under what circumstances?'

'I met her by chance, on the street.'

'I need more details. Did you meet in Paris?'

'Yes, on Boulevard Haussmann, one afternoon when it was

quite windy and the scarf around her neck blew off. I ran to retrieve it and brought it back to her. She thanked me and, since we were going in the same direction, we started walking together.'

'What time was it?'

'Six or so. But it was winter, and it was already dark.'

It seems easy to guess what an older woman is looking for in a young man, with whom she can achieve physical intimacy; but it's not. Because Larten didn't want to mentally review the whole list of typical places, but rather he wanted to imagine something different, now that he was in contact with two relationships of that kind; and also he'd been seduced by the charm and bravery of Irène Duroudier.

'That's how we met. Later she invited me to have a glass of wine in a bar, near the Opera.'

'Which bar?'

'I don't remember. But it was in la Rue Auber. Because we had a drink and she asked for my phone number and then she left the bar. And I turned a little toward the door to watch her as she walked away, and I saw the street sign.'

'How long ago was that?'

'It was January. So almost eight months ago.'

There was something in Gassiat's demeanour, in his careful way of speaking, in his gestures, in what might once have been called his manners, that also fascinated Larten. It certainly didn't fit with the prison environment they were in at that moment, but clearly neither to any other recognisable environment. It was not an imitation of elegance or a pretence of belonging to high society. So, what did it mean?

'But you don't live in Paris. What were you doing there?'

'I had gone to a seminar on contemporary music.'

'What else did you talk about with her?'

'I would never have done her any harm.'

'If I didn't believe you, I wouldn't be here, Émile. What else did you used to talk about?'

He had opened his eyes again and placed his hands as if on

a piano keyboard, visible only to himself.

'The news, and cinema, which she liked very much, and concerts... and cooking... the normal things in life.'

'And in those conversations, did you ever speak to her about the existence of Irène Duroudier?'

'No. We didn't have that kind of open relationship. Nor any other for that matter.'

'Let's go back to the question of location. If you never went to your house, where did you meet up?'

'In hotels or apartments. She took care of making the reservation and asked me to meet her there.'

Just like in Biarritz, Larten thought, which, far from helping, confirmed a dating pattern that further incriminated Gassiat.

'Madame Audiard was apparently a very rich woman. However, the Biarritz apartment where she was found dead was, let's say, of inferior quality. Were the places where she met you like this too?'

'No.'

'Luxury, then?'

'Neither one nor the other. They were places that were fine, elegant and comfortable.'

'I'm going to ask you to make a list of all the ones you remember before you leave.'

'OK.'

'But now, let's go back to the first day. Whereabouts, more or less, on the Boulevard Haussmann did you meet? I want you to understand that, for now, we have nothing to go on. The killer left no trace at the crime scene, and no-one can corroborate your alibi. We have absolutely nothing to prove your innocence. So, all we have left is the street and whether you were seen there. The good news is that I'm a good street detective.'

Émile Gassiat smiled very briefly, just a hint of a smile, and Larten for that instant thought he understood what he was looking for, the key to the bond that united those women with their young lover, far from the typical clichés. But the smile disappeared too quickly, and with it that key.

'I don't remember exactly how far along the Boulevard, but I hadn't walked far from the shop. A few minutes. And we didn't have to walk far to the cafe either. Although with Elisabeth we went more slowly.'

'Well, I'm going back to Paris to try to find out more. To begin with, what could she be doing that day in that neighbourhood quite far from her house. I'll be back as soon as I have any news and if you remember anything, any detail, no matter how small or insignificant it may seem, let me know.'

'I will.'

'And now, please write down all the names you remember of the hotels and apartments where you met.'

Larten held out his pad and fountain pen, and Émile Gassiat began to write. First, he drew a vertical line that divided the page into two halves. The left column for hotels, the right column for apartments. He acted like a diligent, obedient student from a time gone by. A student from an old-fashioned school, with its desks always neatly arranged, and its blackboard, and its windows overlooking a yard with a single tree; and with its steady, secure standards that no one questioned. And perhaps what those women found in Émile, beyond his physical appeal, was precisely his delicate old-fashioned demeanour, that took them back to their own past, to the time of their youth.

Émile finished writing and handed over the notebook.

'I think they're all there.'

'Thank you. I'll be back to visit you soon.'

'I need you to do me a favour.'

'Tell me. What is it?'

'Could you get me a music notebook and some soft pencils?'

'Consider it done.'

'Thank you. My cell is pretty quiet. And silence is a place for music.'

And the phrase sounded to Larten like it had been spoken from a great distance, far away from the place and time that imprisoned them.

4

The Third Woman

Larten entered the café on the Rue Auber, possibly the same one where Elisabeth Audiard and Émile had had their first drink together. It was just past six in the evening, but at the start of September at that time of day it was not yet dark. He ordered a beer. Wine required the kind of attention that he was unable to give at that moment. He was upset and anxious. He had walked the length of the Boulevard Haussmann, up one side and down the other, searching the adjacent avenues and streets. Anjou, Pasquier, Caumartin, Mathurins, Taibout, Havre, Mogador... He had read dozens, maybe hundreds of signs, business names and plates, advertisements... And all this effort was pointless. When you don't know what you're looking for, the streets are empty, despite the crowds of people and the heavy traffic. And even silent, although the incessant chatter would seem to suggest otherwise.

How was he going to work out where Elisabeth Audiard was coming from that evening? Perhaps from a rendezvous with a young lover in a hotel or a nearby apartment? But none of the names that appeared on the list Émile had put together for him were in that area. So where was she coming from? From an appointment with the doctor, the dentist, the hairdresser? From some friends' house?

He ordered another beer. How was he going to find out where she'd been coming from and, in any case, what for?

ANTONIA LASSA

What was the point of searching like this? Nothing seemed to connect Elisabeth Audiard's death with that specific geographical location in Paris. This was only the place where she had got to know Émile Gassiat, who would become her lover, not her killer.

And yet, Larten's intuition, like the needle of a compass indicating magnetic north, insisted on highlighting that point. He left the bar and started walking in no specific direction. Without stopping, he telephoned Irène Duroudier.

'I've seen him in prison; he's fine... No, he's not depressed at all. He asked me for a ruled notebook. According to him, the silence surrounding him in his cell makes room for music... Indeed, as you say, surprisingly mature... I don't know how long, Irène. But it's a delicate matter and right now I have nothing on which to rest my defence. That's why I've called , because I need your help... Try and find out something about the life of Elisabeth Audiard. I'm sure you must have friends or acquaintances in common. Anything that might be useful to us. Some thread that we could start to pull - places she frequently visited, hobbies, any enemies perhaps... Yes, I know it's a delicate matter. But you are the only person that can help us get access to her inner circle. As you can well imagine, they're not going to invite me in.'

Larten had started to go up Rue de Rome, and as he passed a musical instrument shop, he replayed again in his mind the declaration Émile had made before the judge.

He took out his mobile phone and called Madame Duroudier once more.

'I'm sorry to bother you again, Irène. But I need to ask you one more question. Did you give Émile a piano as a present? Thank you.'

*

This time he would take the campervan and head to Bayonne. He needed all his things with him, "within easy reach", as he had told Irène the first day they'd met. Yes, everything close by – his laptop, files, books, not forgetting his small wine cellar... On this trip that he sensed was going to be decisive.

If he left Paris early the following day, he could visit Émile in prison at the start of the afternoon.

It was as if he hadn't moved from his seat since the last time Larten visited him. He had the same good-natured and serene look on his face as always.

'I discovered something in Paris that I need you to confirm right away.'

'I'm listening.'

'You declared before the judge that the piano in your apartment in Arcachon was a gift.'

'That's correct.'

'And that it wasn't Madame Audiard who gave it to you.'

'No.

'I now know it wasn't a gift from Irène either because she just told me that herself in Paris. So, who did buy the piano for you?'

For the first time since they met, Émile Gassiat lowered his gaze.

'Who Émile? Another woman?'

'I'm not going to answer that question.' he looked Larten in the eye once more. 'I can't.'

'I'm your lawyer, you're not before the police or the investigating judge. I don't know how many times you've stated that there wasn't another woman. If you have another friend, I have to know. Do you?'

'I'm not going to answer, I can't.'

'Look Émile, I don't think you realise just how serious the situation is you're in. In principle, you're the only suspect for the murder of Elisabeth Audiard, whose family are very powerful. And I have nothing to be able to get you out of this miserable prison and stop you from rotting in here until the trial, whenever that might be! And what's worse, I have nothing that helps me believe that you will be acquitted.'

'I'm innocent. Sooner or later, you'll be able to prove it.'

'I'm not looking for proof of your innocence, rather I'm searching for a clue that will lead me to real culprit. So, I'm going to put it to you in another way: either you tell me everything, including the name of the person who bought you the piano...'

'I can't.'

'... or I'll stop being your lawyer right now.'

'I swore to them I would tell no-one.'

'I'm sorry, but you'll have to break that promise. In any case you know that I am subject to a duty of confidentiality. Whatever you tell me will remain between the two of us. Who gave you the piano? A woman?'

Émile Gassiat leaned forward. The table between them was so narrow that his face was almost touching Larten's.

'Yes.'

'I need her name and details of how I can find her.'

Émile had returned to his usual upright position, his back pushed up against the back of the chair.

'She's got nothing to do with this. How could she be involved in this horrible matter?'

'You have to give me her name.'

'She's called Mathilde.'

'And her last name?'

Émile covered his mouth with his left hand and shut his eyes. He stayed like this for a few moments. Larten waited patiently, without saying a word.

'I'd rather write it for you,' the young man said at last.

Larten passed him the notebook and fountain pen.

'Does she also live in París?'

'No, in Bordeaux.'

'Write down her address for me as well, if you know it.'

'Yes, I do.'

Émile Gassiat quickly wrote down what he'd been asked for and closed the notebook before returning it to Larten.

'How is it possible that the police haven't linked her to you?'

'Because I've never had her phone number, nor her email address. Nor she mine.'

'So how did you arrange to meet up?'

'We always met at her house. At each meeting she gave me the day and time of the next one.'

'Have you been seeing her for a long time?'

'Two years or so.'

'How did you meet her?'

'At Saint Jean station. I had caught the train in Arcachon and on the way I started composing a small piece of music. When we got to Bordeaux, I sat down at the piano, one of those that they've started putting in railway stations for people to play. *A vous de jouer* they call them, it's your turn to play.'

'Yes, I've seen them.'

'Mathilde had gone to see someone off at the station and she stopped to hear me play. She loves music and art in general.'

'Is she an older woman as well?'

'Yes.'

'Rich too?'

'I guess so. She lives in a beautiful house.'

As he spoke his voice rose slightly, as someone does when faced with beauty, unable to suppress their admiration or joy. And Larten thought he seemed even younger, in his early teens; and he was curious about Emile, about his life and his desires and his feelings that, there in that interview room in Bayonne's bleak, inhospitable Villa Chagrin prison, in a way that he could only describe as desperate.

Who was this young man? Where was he from? What kind of affection and attraction drew him to those women who seemed to have so much in common?

Larten kept repeating the same questions over and over again as he walked back to the river where he'd parked the campervan and later on the drive all the way to Bordeaux.

Yet the third woman was different. Larten had easily found

her number in the telephone directory and had called her at dusk, as soon as he reached Bordeaux. It was she who'd answered.

'Good evening, I'd like to speak with Mathilde'

'Speaking. Who's calling?'

'It's Albert Larten, I'm acting as Émile Gassiat's lawyer, although you probably know him by the name of Maurice Darbo. I need to speak with you.'

'Tomorrow morning at eleven in the entrance hall of the Centre des Arts du Cirque de Bordeaux. There's an interesting exhibition on. Buy yourself the catalogue.'

And she hung up.

She was different. To begin with, she seemed quite a bit younger than the other two women, seventy years old at the most. And she looked different as well, more casual, sporty clothes, short hair, no make-up. Larten hadn't put any make-up on for this meeting either. But he had his high-heeled boots on, and he was holding the exhibition catalogue clearly visible. She recognised him straight away.

'You're Larten, aren't you?'

'Yes.'

'Well, let's go in. I've bought the tickets.'

Larten followed her. In silence they crossed the main hall and took the stairs to the second floor. Definitely different. Larten walked behind her, comparing her with Irène Duroudier, a woman who didn't try to hide her age. On the contrary, she seemed to display her elegant maturity with satisfaction and express it in such a classic manner. Larten wasn't aware what Elisabeth Audiard had been like in life nor how she had lived later in life. There were no photos of her, neither in the report they had given him nor on the internet. Émile didn't have any either. As far as her expensive, unflashy clothes and accessories were concerned, that the police had found intact and neatly organised at the crime scene, they really didn't say much about her. Nor could they deduce anything about her style or the way she expressed herself under the terrible marks that had been left on her body. And that all those involved in the investigation, including Larten himself, interpreted these as the expression of the killer's aberrant "creativity", a kind of artist's signature, the term the coroner had coined, and which was included in the report. Those marks obscenely visible on the body, were like the master strokes of a portrait the perpetrator wanted to paint of himself. Everyone had accepted this hypothesis. But now Larten hesitated, as he went up the stairs, following the steady pace of the woman who so obviously defied any age stereotype. Perhaps they had all been wrong, including himself, in interpreting the acid marks that way. It was Mathilde's physical appearance that suddenly, without any justification or logic, made him rethink the meaning of the drawings on Madame Audiard's skin; rethink even the relevance of describing them as drawings.

They entered a small room where the only light came from a large screen where a film was playing.

'We can sit down here. This video has hardly any sound and I don't think at this time any visitors will disturb us.'

They sat next to each other, in front of the screen where they could see through the intermittence of light and shadow... the flow of a river.

'What interests me is not the end point of what we call contemporary art,' Mathilde said. 'Most of it disappoints me. Rather, it's the starting point. The liberty that today's artists take to get anywhere, in any field.'

Larten was going to take that same liberty too.

'I'm going to be honest with you. I don't know what I'm looking for in coming to see you.'

'Ever since I learned of the murder of that woman, allegedly at the hands of a young man from Arcachon, I knew that someone would come looking for me, that sooner or later, one way or another, they would find me.'

'Did you find out from the press?'

'No. Through social networks. And I mean the more

traditional kind, you know, the tedious litany of friends of friends of other friends...'

'You seem very angry.'

'I am. I'm not happy at all being caught up in this business.'

'You're not involved. Émile has spoken only to me about his relationship with you, and he did so because I put him under a lot of pressure.'

'Under pressure or not, he did it.'

'Because he's in jail, wrongly implicated in the murder.'

'He didn't kill her then?'

'I'm convinced he didn't. You're not? Do you think he's capable of doing something like that?'

'No, how stupid! Of course I don't believe him capable of doing such a thing. The problem is that now I don't believe him where I believed him before, and that changes everything.'

'I forced him to break the promise he had made you to not discuss your relationship with anyone. We are in exceptional circumstances.'

Mathilde was looking at the screen and Larten was looking at her. He watched his face appear and disappear to the rhythm of the film's lighting. And he could also hear the tension in her voice appear and disappear, at the same pace, because in the dark she spoke more slowly and in a more intimate tone.

'No, don't call them that. They are terrible, devastating, tragic circumstances... whatever you want, but not exceptional. On the contrary, totally ordinary... an eternal and pitiful déjà vu...'

'When was the last time you were with Émile?'

'If you want to know if I can provide him with an alibi for the day of the crime, the answer is no. I've spent the whole month of August in Sardinian waters, trapped on a boat with too many people. Anyway, no ship is ever big enough. Fortunately, the sea remains, at certain times, vast and empty, to swim far away.'

'Do you like swimming?'

'Like is not the word. It's something much more intense. In the sea the body is disoriented, it feels as though it's in another world and in another time. Or if you'd rather, swimming is the same as sexual pleasure, being there and being present in its purest form. It's wonderful.'

The screen lit up again, illuminating Mathilde just as she turned her head in the direction of the entrance to the room at the same time as someone came in. It was then then Larten saw a small scar behind her right ear. A small line, very fine and slightly darker than the skin. A tiny stroke and yet with the potential to change everything. Like a sign that suddenly appears on a road that up to that point had been deserted, and along which you have been driving blind. Because everyone had been wrong from the start, Larten told himself, including himself.

'Let's get out of here,' Mathilde said when the visitor that had just come in took a few steps and sat down near them, 'in any case, I've seen this work so many times.'

Larten followed her back to the stairs, which they began to slowly descend.

'I need to ask you something else, Mathilde.'

'What?'

'Something of a more personal nature.'

'Because what you've asked me so far doesn't seem very personal to you.'

'Have you had surgery? I mean cosmetic surgery.'

'And you, Mr. Larten, do you pluck your eyebrows?'

'A little yes, very discreetly.'

'Not so discreetly, since I noticed it.'

'Because you know what to look for. Like me, who noticed the small scar behind you ear.'

'Yes, it's still visible. It's taking its time to disappear; but it will.'

Larten stopped and sat down on one of the steps on the stairs. Mathilde kept going down, but immediately retraced her steps and sat down beside him.

'I don't think it's of any interest to your case whether or not I have had cosmetic surgery.'

But Larten knew she was wrong. In the same way that he was able to anticipate the promise of a great wine, when tasting a grape must, he knew that that small scar represented an enormous progress in his investigation.

'Believe me, it can help us a lot. I'm sure now. Has a French doctor ever operated on you? From Bordeaux or maybe from Paris?'

'No. I only have treatment in the United States. As far away as possible from here. Here everybody knows your business. Everything ends up being common knowledge. I'm sorry I can't give you the name of someone within easy reach.'

'Don't worry, you've already helped me a lot.'

'Are you going to get him out of prison soon?'

'Yes, I hope so, soon.'

And he wasn't lying. He already felt that he was in possession of a valuable clue.

'How soon?'

'I don't know, but I'm going to do everything in my power to make it happen as soon as possible.'

'It is our bodies that age, Albert, not us. We remain the same inside, with the same desire. And that tension becomes unbearable at times. Try to get him out of jail as soon as possible. Yes, do everything that's in your power.'

Mathilde got up. Larten was going to do the same, but she stopped him.

'No, don't come with me now. Let me go alone.'

'Ok, I'll let you know when it's all over.'

'No need, I'll find out myself.'

She went down the stairs, reached the exit and disappeared.

Larten waited a few minutes, then left the museum and headed for the parking lot. He got in the campervan and pulled the photographs of Elisabeth Audiard that the forensic police had taken at the scene of the crime from the case file. He placed them side by side on his desk.

They had all been mistaken from the beginning, including himself. They had allowed themselves to be seduced by the forensic officer's interpretation, surely because it contained an enigma to decipher, a code, the hieroglyph that formed those drawings on the dead woman's skin. And it's difficult to resist the intellectual challenge a hieroglyph represents, and the rivalry it immediately creates among those who discover it. Who will be the smartest, the one who manages to decipher it first, reveal the hidden message before anyone else and solve the case? They had all been carried away by this double seduction, including himself. But now Larten saw his mistake. It had been enough for him to follow the line marked by Mathilde's small scar, to realise this.

Those marks on the corpse were not drawings, they weren't a new form writing to be read. They weren't inscribed on the victim's skin to convey a message. How had he not thought this before? They were there for the complete opposite, to cover up that message, to silence what Elisabeth Audiard's skin had to say. What had to be discovered, what had to be read and what the murderer had tried to destroy with acid, was what lay beneath those horrific markings that the scientific police's photographs reproduced, with cruel precision.

Before leaving for Paris, he called the prison at Bayonne. He had to wait more than twenty minutes but, in the end, he was put through to his client.

'Émile, do you know if Elisabeth had undergone any cosmetic surgery or been to a cosmetic surgeon?'

'Not that I know of, no.'

'Did she never talk to you about any skin treatment she'd had?'

'No, I don't remember.'

'Did she have any particular marks or wounds on her skin the last time you saw her?'

'Nothing that particularly caught my attention. Older people have skin... how can I say... very lived-in.'

Larten was sorry that Émile was on the other end of the

phone. He would have liked to be in front of him right then, to show him with a look or a small gesture, the emotion that his words produced. A lived-in skin, yes, an entire city in the skin, footsteps, voices, welcoming places, and also the elements.

'But are you sure you didn't find something different, unusual on her skin? Try to remember, it's extremely important.'

'No, nothing that surprised me. Have you already had that interview in Bordeaux?'

'Yes. And everything went very well, don't worry. Now I am going back to Paris. I want to investigate something. I'll be back to see you as soon as possible. Bye for now.'

'Wait a minute Mr. Larten, don't hang up. I just remembered one thing. The last time we met, in June, Elisabeth told me that she didn't like summer, that she had to protect herself constantly from the sun. "And even more so now," she had added.'

'Didn't you ask what she meant, what that "now" meant?'

'No, because when she said it, she was looking at me and smiling, and I thought I'd understood.'

5

Skin

Larten unfolded the map of the eighth arrondissement and held it in place on the table with two paperweights. With a red marker, he drew a vertical line along the Boulevard Haussmann, from the point where the Berteil store is located, from where Émile had gone out after changing his jersey, to the intersection of Haussmann with Rue Auber, which Madame Audiard and Émile had already travelled together. Then he joined the two ends of that line with a semicircle from the left; they had found on the odd-numbered side of the boulevard, Madame Audiard must have surely come from there. She was an old woman; she couldn't have walked a long distance. Perhaps she'd just left the house she'd visited. She'd not even finished wrapping her scarf around her neck.

Inside the semicircle that Larten had just drawn there were only a few streets: Anjou, Mathurins, Pasquier, Arcade... Larten had already walked round these on his first wander through the neighbourhood, but he didn't know what he was looking for then. This time, he did.

He searched the internet but couldn't find the address of a plastic surgeon or dermatologist in any of those streets. And yet he knew he had to hold on to that clue. Skin was the key to the whole thing; he was convinced it.

He put away the map. He had to go back to that neighbourhood and go door to door, like a conscientious viticulturist walks through his vineyard, observing the detail of each bunch.

He started at Berteil and set off down Boulevard Haussmann, in the direction of the Opera. At the corner of rue d'Anjou he turned right and then walked slowly, down both sides of the street. He didn't find any professional signs or plaques that could help him.

He was once again on the Boulevard, but Émile had to have met Madame Audiard further down. He went back along Anjou and on reaching the Rue des Mathurins turned left. He walked down on the same side, slowly, stopping at each doorway. He reached the Rue Pasquier, crossed over and continued along Mathurins... and then he saw on a facade, on the lower part of a row of business plaques of different sizes and materials, half hidden by the refuse bin that was against the wall, a brass rectangle bearing the inscription *Dermatology. 3rd floor*. The building was located quite close to the rue de l'Arcade which immediately led to Boulevard Haussmann. That was the route that Elisabeth Audiard must have followed before meeting with Émile who was walking briskly down the boulevard, on the same side of the pavement.

He couldn't be certain about this yet, but as he stood before that brass plaque Larten felt the same sense of triumph that an archaeologist must feel when he suddenly discovers, among the thousands of fragments of a vessel, a different piece, a sliver of bone, a coin, a tiny yet highly promising shard of a mosaic.

The door was open and there was an elevator, but Larten preferred to go up the stairs. He needed to calm down, settle the emotion caused by this discovery, so that his heart that he felt beating in his throat calmed down. He paused on the second-floor landing to remove Monique's silk scarf that he often wore under his shirt and wrapped it visibly around his neck. Clothing suitable for the visit he was about to make.

On one of the two doors on the third floor, a small wooden sign declared, F. Arbogast. Dermatology. The office doorbell didn't work. Larten knocked, once, twice, the third time harder. Finally, a man with completely white hair but whose face looked no more than forty years old opened the door a crack.

'Can I help you?'

'I'm here for a consultation. Are you Dr. Arbogast?'

'Yes, but I'm not seeing clients right now, sorry. My secretary is gone and until I find her replacement, the practice will remain closed.'

'It's important, urgent actually.'

'I'm sorry but I can't help you.'

They had spoken through the door that was barely ajar. Larten had only been able to distinguish the end of a desk on which a large cardboard box was open, the kind that are used for removals. The doctor was already closing the door when Larten spoke up, raising his voice slightly.

'It is very important to me. Your practice was recommended to me by a friend, Madame Audiard.'

The movement of the door stopped.

'Audiard?'

'Yes, Elisabeth Audiard. A good friend.'

'The name means nothing to me.'

'Wasn't she a patient of yours?'

'Off the top of my head, I really can't say. Maybe my secretary, she's the one who takes care of the files, well she used to, before she left me stranded with no word of warning because, apparently, she has found a much better job in the Cote d'Azur. Of course, there's no shortage of work in dermatology there, what with the sun and all that...'

It was obvious that he was trying to change the conversation.

'Wasn't she a patient of yours?' Larten insisted.

'She left me stranded. That's why I have the office closed and I'm not able see you.'

'Didn't Madame Audiard come here then?'

Larten had intentionally put all the questions in the past

tense, waiting for a doctor to slip up, which didn't happen.

'I've already answered that that name means nothing to me. That means she's not a patient at this practice. I would remember. Maybe she attended the clinic.'

'Do you also see clients at a clinic?'

'Of course. Cochard Clinical Centre. Call there if you want an appointment.'

'What happened to your secretary?'

'Happened? Absolutely nothing has happened to her, except that she has gone to the Cote d'Azur overnight, forcing me to close the practice. You just don't do that.'

And the indignation in his voice sounded so clear, so convincing, that Larten thought that if the doctor were lying, he was an actor, one of the good ones, and therefore would be a tough nut to crack. Before Arbogast closed the door completely, Larten had time to ask him, 'Your name, doctor, please? This F on the plaque, what does it correspond to? Elisabeth didn't tell me. It's so I can make an appointment.'

'Francis. And you're right to ask, because there's another doctor Arbogast who works at the clinic, that has nothing to do with me.'

And with that, he closed the door.

Larten went into a nearby cafe. The place was almost empty, and he was able to sit at a table far from the bar, from where he had a perfect view of the doorway the doctor would come out of. He called Monique.

'Hello beautiful, I need to ask you a favour. I need you to give me a ride.'

'But you know I prefer it when you take control.'

'Not always, you're right. I see you're in a good mood.'

'I need your motorcycle, with you on it, of course, for something that I'll explain to you when you get here. Are you going to help me or not?'

'In the cafe on the corner of Mathurins and Pasquier. As soon as you can.'

Monique didn't take long to arrive, parking the bike near

the entrance to the café. From where he was sitting, Larten signalled for her to wait for him outside and went out to meet her.

'I'd rather we talk out here,' he said as he went to kiss her.

'What's up, Albert?'

'I need you to follow someone for me. I can't with the campervan, and it doesn't seem wise to do so by taxi.'

'Who is it?'

'A doctor who has his surgery a few doors up. When he comes out, I'll indicate to you who it is. I can't be sure, but something tells me he's involved in the Biarritz crime. Come on, let's go inside now.'

But Monique didn't have time to drink her coffee. First, they saw a taxi arrive, stopping just in front of the doorway to Arbogast's surgery. The doctor came out immediately holding a cardboard box under his left arm, bulky but apparently not very heavy.

'That's him. Be very careful, my love; and make sure he doesn't catch sight of you, so he doesn't suspect anyone is following him. If he is who I think he is, he's dangerous and I also believe that he'll be quite uneasy after my visit. I'll wait for you at home.'

'No way. You're coming with me'

'I can't do that. You know that getting on that motorcycle terrifies me. What's more, the doctor has already seen me.'

'Without that scarf around your neck and with your helmet on, he won't recognise you even if he notices the bike.'

'Do you have another helmet?'

'You know I always take a spare one for you. Because I love your spontaneity.'

Monique was definitely in a great mood, and Larten couldn't delay. The taxi had already set off.

Dr. Arbogast didn't seem aware that he was being followed. He got out of the taxi near Trocadéro, calmly walked towards a refuse bin, dumped the contents of the box there, but kept the cardboard that he folded carefully under his arm all the way to Avenue Georges Mandel, where he went into an elegant building. Monique stopped a little way off and raised the visor on her helmet. Turning to Larten she asked, 'How was the ride?'

'Better than I expected. You drive very well, darling, and I was concentrating so much on not losing sight of him, that I didn't have time to think about anything else. If our doctor lives in that house, things must be going pretty well for him.'

'Quite.'

Without doubt many distinguished patients, such as Madame Audiard, Larten thought. Everything seemed to make sense and fall into place since he had begun to follow the trail of the skin: a dermatological surgery located close to the place where Elisabeth and Émile first met – a missing secretary, a doctor disposing of the contents of a box away from his work, and brutal marks on the face, neck, belly of the victim. These were not isolated elements. but rather pieces of an interlocking puzzle that joined together perfectly. They aren't random elements, Larten said to himself, but pearls that are already strung on an invisible thread, forming a necklace.

'Arbogast has taken great care to dispose of the contents of that box. I'd like to take a look inside that refuse bin. Can you take me over there?'

To distract from his nervousness during the motorcycle ride, Larten kept repeating to himself a phrase from his beloved Flaubert. It is not the pearls that make the necklace but the thread. He had to concentrate on retrieving that thread, to rebuild the story of Elisabeth Audiard's murder, resolutely and convincingly, point by point.

He lifted the lid of the refuse bin. It was practically empty and the things that were no doubt the contents of the doctor's box lay scattered far from Larten's range. The bin was a large container with four wheels, the bottom of which was unattainable even for someone of his height. It would be necessary to push it over. But that would make a noise that would alarm the neighbours and no doubt raise police suspicion, and anyway, the garbage collection truck wasn't far away. Arbogast must have checked the pickup times, before emptying the box.

'Monique, hold the lid for a moment, please, and shine the torch from your mobile inside. I want to see what there is and take some photos.'

At first glance, there were just office supplies, pens, pencils, different coloured felt-tip pens, envelopes, a stapler, a shower of paperclips, post-it pads, a pair of scissors, a ceramic mug that had been smashed, one of the fragments containing a large V, a pencil holder, notebooks...

There was nothing particularly interesting nor anything that really spoke to him, just the boring contents of a work desk, that of the secretary no doubt, the edge of which Larten had caught a glimpse of through the half-open door of Arbogast's surgery. Why would the doctor want to get rid of such mundane material? Was he thinking of permanently closing the surgery and, if so, why? And why dispose of simple office supplies so far from the office? He'd had to take a taxi. Unless he'd simply taken the taxi home and taken the spontaneous decision to get rid of the contents of the box on the way. But why not get the taxi to wait for him in that case? So that the driver wouldn't see him tipping out the contents? Too many unanswered questions on account of a few notebooks, pencils and boxes of staples. Larten took various photographs of the inside of the container with his mobile. He could analyse them later in more detail on the computer.

'Thank you, Monique. Stand back a bit, I'm going to close the lid.'

As he slowly lowered the lid so as not to make a noise, something reached him that had been there all along, but all his attention had been devoted to the contents of desk and he'd forgotten about this – the smell of garbage. A disgusting, cloying smell, but subtle. Just a hint of this stench in the air. The mountain of rubbish that had caused it had disappeared.

Only the trace of it remained, like a boot's imprint of in the mud. And Larten thought his investigation was in a similar position, on the point of turning sour but the rot nowhere to be seen, yet its nauseating smell had already reached him. He carefully closed the container.

'Should I take you home or are you staying with me tonight?' Monique asked.

'With you, of course, my love. But first I'd like us to take a spin on a motorcycle through Paris. Through the Paris of beautiful monuments and dreams.'

The horror was drawing closer but hadn't yet reached him; it was a moment to pause, to call a truce, and Larten wanted to fill that moment with beauty.

'You don't know how happy it makes me that you've suggested we do this.'

'Yes, I know, and that's precisely why I'm asking you.'

*

Larten stroked Monique's bare back as she lay sleeping beside him. The skin was the human body's largest organ, and it was strewn with innumerable sensitive receptors that made it a magnificent terrain for pleasure and knowing, because the skin was often the first warning and first reaction to the environment around us, not only to the outside world but also in our most intimate moments. A sudden blush or a shiver instantly alerts us to things that take time to comprehend and process. That's why the skin can also become our worst enemy, Larten thought. When all those sensitive receptors are turned off like melted light bulbs, they no longer emit any signal and leave us defenceless and ignorant as we face the world. Or they harm us with a powerful shock at the slightest touch because when the skin is too worn, it can no longer protect us and we are left naked, afraid, stripped bare like live wires.

To look after the skin was to preserve pleasure, to prolong it. That's what Elisabeth Audiard had sought in Dr. Arbogast's surgery, more time for pleasure with her young lover. But it had cost her life. Larten had very few elements to go on and nothing to prove it and yet he knew he wasn't wrong. And perhaps, he told himself, what we call intuition is precisely that. An invisible skin that surrounds us, covered with such extraordinarily sensitive sensors, that it perceives danger before we do.

Larten downloaded the photographs he had taken of the inside of the refuse container onto his computer. He began reviewing them on screen. There was nothing he hadn't already seen, notebooks, pencils, staples, the V on a fragment of the broken cup, loose sheets of paper that had become dirty from contact with the bottom of the refuse bin. He zoomed in a bit to examine them in more detail. And then he noticed a small area, lighter in tone, surrounded by staples, paper clips, envelopes, and post-it pads of different colours and sizes. Larten expanded the image a bit more. What he saw was a minuscule fragment of the back of a postcard... he could make out a few letters, handwritten in blue, arranged in two lines on the spacing usually kept for writing the address.

And if that postcard was from off the secretary's desk, it was surely because it belonged to her, because she had wanted to keep it there for some reason, because she liked the scenery on the front, that no one could appreciate anymore, or due to the relationship she had with the person who had sent it... That postcard had nothing to do with Arbogast, but rather with his secretary. It was the first contact with that woman who had vanished overnight and who Larten needed to find as soon as possible.

He began to copy the letters that were still visible into a notebook. On the first line, where the name is normally written was "ie Ri" and what looked like a "b". In the second line, where the address is usually goes, "e Pie".

The mug fragment found in the refuse bin bore the initial V. So, the woman might be called Valérie or Virginie or Véronique...Rib. As for the address, you could imagine something like Rue Pie... Larten called his friend Edouard Laborde at the Digital Research Institute.

'I have work for your data boffin. I need to find a name and address from a few letters, ... Yes, most likely in Paris. I'll send you what I've managed to recover right away by email.'

'Thanks.'

The answer was not long in coming: Valérie Riboust, 140 Rue Pierre Larousse, 14th Arrondissement.

*

Someone had gone into number 140 and Larten hurriedly grabbed the door so it wouldn't close again. He waited a few minutes and entered the building. He easily found the name on the mailboxes: V. Riboust' 4th floor. He took the elevator. Two doors opened onto the landing. Next to the one on the left there was a child's buggy. He rang the other doorbell. And again, more persistently. Then the door to the neighbouring flat opened, and a young woman appeared, wearing a raincoat and with a baby in her arms.

'Good morning, I'm a friend of Valérie's, I need to talk to her. It appears she's not at home. Do you know what time she usually comes back? I need to talk to her, it's quite important.'

'I haven't seen her in several weeks. Actually, now that I think about it, I haven't seen her all summer.'

'Did she say goodbye to you?'

'Goodbye, no. Why? Was she going somewhere?'

'Exactly how long has it been since you've seen her?'

'Since June. I remember very well because it was my eldest son's last day of class. I met her in the doorway and because I was loaded with lots of stuff, she helped me carry my school things. After that I don't remember seeing her again.'

'Didn't she tell you she was thinking of moving?'

'No.'

'I'm going to be honest, Mrs...'

'Mora.'

'Valérie and I have been friends for a long time, and we see each other every time I come to Paris. This time I can't find her, I called her I don't know how many times on the phone but no answer. I have tried to find her at work, but also with no joy.'

'How strange!'

'Yes. And I'm very worried. Do you happen to have a copy of the keys to her apartment so you can go in and see if there's anything inside to tell us where she is?'

'No, I don't have a copy of her keys and besides, I have to leave now. I'm late.'

'I am extremely worried Mrs Mora. Please help me.'

'I can't. I already told you I don't have her keys.'

'Don't you know of anyone who might have a copy?'

'Perhaps the woman who comes to clean the entrance and the stairs. I know some neighbours leave her their keys, just in case.'

'Where can I find her?'

'She lives at number 132 on this same street. She also takes care of the cleaning there. Madame Pons.'

'Thank you very much.'

Madame Pons lived on the ground floor. She was a robust woman, you could see she was used to physical work; and the same firmness you could see in her naked arms, despite the cold, was there in her character as well.

'I've already told you, no. If people trust me with the keys to their houses, it's not for me to pass them on to the first person who arrives, no matter how worried they are or how much a friend of the family they are.'

'What if, in addition to being a friend of the family, he is responsible for, shall we say, a delicate investigation?'

'What does that mean?'

'That this is an extremely serious matter, Mrs. Pons; and I'm not asking you to give me the keys, but to go into Mrs. Riboust's apartment yourself, to see what we find.'

'To see what I can find because you're not going in.'

'OK, I'll stay outside, on the landing, and I'll tell you what to look for.'

'Oh, because I'm not able to look for myself.'

'This is a very serious matter... and naturally I will repay you for your invaluable help.'

'What does that mean?'

'Fifty euros.'

'I just can't see what you mean.'

'One hundred.'

Madame Pons did not yield in the matter. Larten would stay outside, on the landing, although he could pass on his instructions through the open door.

'Look in the refrigerator and look for the expiry date of the products. Open the washing machine. And the cabinets. And the pantry. Check how the plants are doing if there are any. Is there dust on the furniture?'

Mrs. Pons's report left no room for doubt.

'Clothes put away neatly in the cupboards. The washing machine half-full. The fruit and vegetables kept outside the fridge, completely rotten. The ones inside, rotten or past the expiry date. Dust had gathered for several weeks. All plants dead.'

This was not the apartment of someone who was moving out, but of someone who left home in the morning, hoping to return later. But someone who wasn't coming back anymore.

Larten settled down in the campervan. First, he bought a ticket for the 13.45 flight to Biarritz. Then, he called Madame Duroudier.

'Yes, Irène, I've made quite good progress. I'm travelling to Biarritz this afternoon to meet with the Inspector in charge of the case. But, before I go, I would like to know if the name Francis Arbogast means anything to you. He's a dermatologist and maybe a plastic surgeon too. So, it doesn't ring a bell?' he asked. 'No, I'd prefer it if you didn't make inquiries; I'm afraid that rumours would get out that we're investigating him.'

He also called the Bayonne Serious Crime Squad. Inspector

Canonne would receive him, barring any unforeseen events, late in the afternoon.

*

That red earring in Larten's ear was like a pebble you drop into the water, thought Inspector Canonne, small and yet capable of transforming the whole pond. A small deep-red stone, perhaps a real ruby, was enough to change the lawyer's facial features, disturbing and bewildering Canonne to the point that he couldn't stand it. Maybe because he couldn't deny those feelings, put them away inside, as before. It was as if he were the pond that the stone in Larten's ear had churned up.

'What is it you want?'

'I've come to see you because I've a clue that I think you should investigate, and which will clear my client of any involvement in the murder of Madame Audiard.'

'You seem rather convinced of Gassiat's innocence. Well, you would, wouldn't you, in your position?'

'And it's what yours should be too, Inspector. You should know better than anyone that the accusations against him won't hold and that...'

'Financially maintained by the victim, with no alibi, the author of drawings very similar to those found on the body, operating under a false identity...'

'It's my turn to interrupt you now, Canonne. To begin with, Darbo is not exactly a false name, since it's Émile's mother's last name and therefore also his. As for the rest, no concrete proof, just guesses. I insist, you know very well that there is nothing conclusive against him, and that it's the circumstances of the case and the state the victim was in – which are, well, let's call them unusual – that have led to him being put in jail. I know perfectly well who Elisabeth Audiard was, and who Irène Duroudier is.'

'And the role that Gassiat played in their lives.'

'Yes, but that's not a crime. It may even be the opposite of a crime.'

'Well, Larten, let's leave that, all right? I have no time to waste on this kind of absurd debate. What have you specifically come to see me about?'

Almost ten years had passed since their last meeting, but Larten had changed very little. He'd just gained some weight. But he didn't have a single grey hair. Impeccable teeth too. Although you could never be sure about teeth, they could be his own or perfect implants. The Inspector had finally accepted the resin-bonded replacement tooth that would be ready in a couple of weeks. 'With its advantages and disadvantages,' the dentist had said. But he was certain that it was safe, and that this time his mouth wasn't going to reject the new tooth. It was going to fit just like the rest of his teeth. There was no more open injury to the gum, only a hard hole between the teeth.

'I'd like to remind you, Inspector, Gassiat is not the murderer. So, there's someone still at large and, you can't rule out the chance of them killing again. Maybe another woman like Elisabeth Audiard.'

'A long journey from Paris, for just a few meagre guesses, Larten. It's quite disappointing. Don't you have anything else?'

There was no more hurt. Everything ended up healing or at least closing up. He spoke on the phone with Laure from time to time and managed to get the pain to lessen each time, or rather, to lose a little bit of hope with every call. A triumph. Ten years earlier it had been Larten who had won the trial they were both involved in, but that had been a fairly simple case. He could barely remember it. Now they were faced with something much more complex.

'Yes. I have reason to believe that Madame Audiard was a patient of a dermatologist, Dr. Francis Arbogast. And that she had just left his surgery, in Rue des Mathurins, when she met Émile Gassiat.'

Canonne only vaguely remembered that case. Larten on the other hand remembered it very well, and also the irony he had wielded against him, once the trial was over, to try to demean him, to detract from his standing as a lawyer and the quality of his work. As they were leaving the court, without really knowing what caused him to do so, he'd asked Larten: 'Mr or Mrs Larten?'

But he had had to stop right on the verge of being ironic, unable to achieve his goal, like a cyclist who hits the wall and has to abandon the ascent still far from the top. A failure. Because Larten had replied, 'If you are referring to my parents, they are both perfectly fine. Thank you for asking. It is very kind of you.'

He hadn't known how to respond. And now Larten was sitting in front of him, tall, well built, resounding in his masculinity and yet attractive, disturbingly feminised by that ruby in his left ear; and the Inspector felt a sense of shame for his reaction back then, ten years ago, after he had lost the trial. And that old feeling of guilt was quickly added to the others in his head, and it all had to do with Laure. Laure who perhaps loved him, who would have liked to stay with him, but whom he had driven away from his side because of his clumsiness, his lack of attention, his selfish outbursts, like that day with Larten, *sir or madame*, all of which pointed to his immaturity, his inability to accept being questioned, being vulnerable, losing. Just like the hole in his mouth that resisted being filled, because its function was precisely to remain empty, so his tongue could pass over it again and again, and each time understand the meaning of that absence.

'I've been to see Dr. Arbogast. He says that he does not know any Elisabeth Audiard, that she wasn't his patient. But I am convinced he's lying.'

'And is there is no-one at the surgery who can confirm it or check in the records? A secretary or a nurse, for example. Haven't you talked with anyone else?'

'That's exactly the question, Inspector. There is no

secretary because the woman who held that post, Valérie Riboust, has disappeared.'

'What do you mean she's disappeared?'

'According to the doctor, she took the snap decision to move to the Côte d'Azur because she'd found a better job there. But I've been to her flat.'

'I hope you haven't raided her home.'

Larten smiled and the Inspector wanted to forget about his missing tooth, and do the same, but he didn't dare.

'No, I didn't even go in the flat. It was the concierge who has a copy of the keys. And what she found inside doesn't suggest someone moving house at all. It's the flat of someone who leaves his house to come back, but they don't come back, probably because they can't. There's a thick layer of dust, dead plants, rotten food, clothes getting dirty, mould in a washing machine that hasn't been put on in a long time... And the neighbour on Valérie Riboust's landing hasn't seen her all summer.'

'Any trace of violence in the flat?'

'Apparently not. The concierge would have noticed. But you need to go there and do a thorough search. I can't go any further, now it's over to you.'

'What makes you think the doctor is involved in the disappearance of that woman?'

'He's emptying the surgery. And I think he's lying when he talks about the secretary's move and also when he denies that Madame Audiard was his patient. I think you have to investigate this dermatologist because the key to the case is in the skin. The Biarritz killer left no drawings on the body of his victim. We were all wrong from the beginning. He didn't want to put anything on the skin, rather to do just the opposite: remove, erase the traces of something that was there before, that he had put there before. I am convinced, but I have no means to go further in that research. From now on it is the responsibility of the police.'

'Have you spoken with our forces in Paris?'

'No. I wanted to see you first. You can report the disappearance of Valérie Riboust to the Paris crime squad and establish from the outset a link between the two investigations. But time is short, Inspector. naturally I want my client out of prison as soon as possible. Also, right now I'm thinking mostly about Dr. Arbogast. I turned up at his surgery, and I asked about Madame Audiard. If he's implicated in her death, he already knows someone is investigating him, and he's going to try...'

'To get rid of as much proof as he can.'

'As soon as possible.'

It makes sense, the Inspector said to himself, that the key to the matter lies in the skin. Elisabeth Audiard had been killed without brutality, but her skin had been brutally assaulted. What had been done to her skin was the outrage of this crime, the distinctive sign of his perversion. And it also made sense, therefore, that the murderer was a dermatologist, a skin specialist, someone who knows her inside out, bit by bit; someone who knows how to read all the messages conveyed by the skin and therefore also delete them at will. It made sense. Maybe Larten was right, once again. Ten years ago, he had been up against him and had lost. But now the lawyer was an ally. The clue about the doctor could be the good one, the one that would allow him to put a stop finally to the Biarritz murderer and solve the case. And get away from his own obsession with failure – sir or madame; and 'Good evening, Laure, how's everything going? I miss you.' But Laure never responded to that part of the sentence.

'OK Mr. Larten, I'm going to trust you and talk to my colleagues in Paris. But you have to tell me everything you've done so far and everything you know.'

'Of course. I've prepared a detailed report with everything I've managed to find out about Arbogast. Here it is.'

Larten took a large envelope out of his leather briefcase and handed it to the Inspector.

'You'll see that I've included some photographs in the

report. I took them, two days ago, of the refuse bin where the doctor had just dumped the contents of his secretary's desk.'

'All right, let's look at all this carefully. Are you staying for some time in Bayonne?'

'No, I'm leaving tomorrow. I'll go visit my client in jail, and then take the last flight to Paris.'

The policeman led him to the booth where his client was waiting for him. More than anything, youth is this, Larten thought as soon as he saw Émile through the glass, the extraordinary capacity of the body to quickly expel traces, remnants, just as the sea closes immediately and without leaving the effects of a wake as a ship ploughs on. Because there was that young man, sitting, waiting for him with the same serenity as always, his face unaltered and showing no sign of resentment or weariness, and the same skin, untouched by lack of sleep or poor food.

He got up to shake hands.

'How are you, Émile?'

'I'm fine, don't worry. It's better than I'd imagined. To be honest, I'd never imagined the inside of a prison. But I can work here and that's what matters to me now. Soon I'll need more paper. Would you be so kind as to get me some more ruled notebooks?'

'Yes, I'll do that. But I hope you won't have the chance to use them in here. We're currently following a lead that seems significant. Last time I asked you about Madame Audiard's skin.'

'Yes, I remember. And I've been thinking about it a lot.'

'Skin seems to be the key to this whole matter, Émile. Have you remembered anything that can help us?'

'No, Mr. Larten, and I'm sorry. An older woman's skin is something very complex. A fascinating, exquisite score, but one that cannot be played. Too many notes and too close together. It's not made to be thought about but rather to be felt, I don't know how to express it, a skin you understand when you see it and touch it but that later you can't remember.'

'Yes, I think I understand what you mean.'

Émile leaned forward and lowered his voice even more:

'And in Bordeaux, everything went well? Tell me something else, please.'

'Yes, everything went very well. And it is precisely that meeting that has put us on the right track, and that's going to get you out of here very soon.'

'And then? Maybe she doesn't want to see me anymore.'

That was also a characteristic of youth, Larten told himself, to be able to suffer without it showing on the outside, because the signs of that suffering are like plants that are still too timid, too tender to break the surface.

'I think she will. She values her freedom too much not to understand that you have to defend yours. And she also likes your music.'

'Did she tell you that?'

Émile looked at him without a trace of sadness in his eyes, like a sea that is calm once more.

'You told me yourself. That she had stopped, the first day at the Gare Saint Jean, to hear you play the piano. I'm going to buy those lined notebooks before returning to Paris. They will bring them right away. Keep making good music and she will want to stay close to you.'

'I hope so.'

6

Hirondelle

Just like every time when he went out at night, Francis Arbogast took his wife's car, the Peugeot Tepee with its tinted windows, that Evelyne used to go on her bird-watching trips.

They'd had dinner and then made love as usual, then he had gone out looking for one of those prostitutes on Rue Saint Denis. This is how it was, those nights when he was out on the prowl increased his desire for his wife, probably because what was waiting for him later was an intimacy with a female body for which he wouldn't feel the slightest attraction and that would give him no pleasure.

Every time he had to go out, he pretended to have some emergency or other at the clinic.

'I must go. The patient is very old and her injuries have become infected. I think we're getting the treatment right but tonight it's vital I attend to her. I prefer to be there and supervise everything myself.'

'Are you going to stay long?'

Arbogast knew that he had a task ahead of him that would undoubtedly keep him occupied all night.

'I'm afraid so. It's a delicate case. It might take all night.'

'Fine, but do try and rest a little.'

'Yes, I'll try.'

He took the usual precaution, although he knew it was unnecessary because Evelyne never called him at work.

'If something comes up and you need to contact me, send me a text, don't call the clinic's switchboard.'

Dr. Arbogast loved driving around Paris at night, the traffic flowed freely. Above all, the chiaroscuro cast by the streetlights. For him, the shadows so clearly distinct from the light, seemed like a problem waiting to be solved. Or like a poison that came with its own antidote. The whole effect gave him confidence and courage. There was no room for doubt. Just what he needed to get the job done.

He wasn't disturbed by the visit from that man that afternoon who had wanted to ask him questions about Elisabeth. A strange-looking man. Effeminate? No, he wouldn't say that, but confused yes, unclear. This undoubtedly indicated a fluid sexuality, a salty, sweet mix. A sexuality of excess, he said out loud. And this very expressive conclusion pleased him and made him smile. This man's visit had naturally disturbed him, but not unsettled him. He had nothing left to fear. Elisabeth wasn't registered at the practice and Valerie was no longer there to confirm that he had treated her.

He turned left and started down Rue Brillat-Savarin. It was an advantage that the entrance to the garage was via that street which was narrower and more unobtrusive than the Rue de Rungis, where the main entrance to the house was. The automatic door opened noiselessly – he kept the mechanism in perfect working order.

He wasn't worried, but he knew that he had to deal with this matter as soon as possible. And then continue with his research more discreetly; perhaps wait several months before carrying out new trials.

He went up to the first floor where he'd set up the laboratory and his bedroom. There he undressed and put on the casual clothes he always wore on his nightly outings. He put on a wig and dark contact lenses that concealed perfectly his blue eyes, and picked up the walking cane. If someone had to describe the man who some nights came to the Rue Saint

Denis, one of the few places where elderly prostitutes could be found, they would have said, dark hair, brown eyes and a slight limp in his right leg.

He went down to the ground floor where there was a kitchen, a bathroom, a living room, and a second bedroom that had been set up to receive the women. This house was perfect, exactly what he needed. It even had a little garden in the back, where two leafy trees shielded him from the prying eyes of the neighbours. It was also surrounded by a wall that was high enough to keep him from being seen or heard from the street. He got in the car; opened the garage door and drove out. The Rue Brillat-Savarin was perfectly deserted.

Rosa was in her usual spot, illuminated by the garish lights of a sex shop. Dr. Arbogast limped over to her. The woman greeted him with a nod of the head, and started up the street; but he stopped her.

'Wait. Today we are not going to your house but to mine. I have the car parked a little bit further on, a small grey Peugeot van. I'll be waiting for you at the corner of the Rue de Metz in fifteen minutes, not before.'

'Is everything else the same as usual?'

'Yes.'

'All night and just to sleep?'

'Yes, the same as usual. Just to sleep.'

'I don't have the pills with me, I'll have to go get them before I meet you.'

'I have the same ones at home. But anyway, you'll have plenty of time with fifteen minutes to get them.'

He told her to sit in the back seat, where the tinted windows of the car were darker and no-one would see her from the street, even if they got quite close to the car.

He'd finish off the job tonight and then he'd put a stop to everything. He would stop going to Rue de Rungis laboratory for a while. Although it was highly unlikely that they'd connect him to that house, as he hadn't signed any rental contract and he'd paid in cash for more than two years. The owner wasn't the least bit interested in making this deal common knowledge.

They hadn't spoken on the way, but before they reached the entrance to Rue Brillat-Savarin, Arbogast asked the woman, 'I haven't seen Nina in a long time, do you know anything about her?'

'No-one's seen her for ages. It seems she got sick and left.'

'Sick, in what way?'

'I don't know. An infection, I think. Something serious for her to have stopped work.'

So that's what they were saying, an infection. It suited him that Nina's friends and acquaintances thought that. Yes, an infection, a sexually transmitted disease the ravages of which were already showing although she tried hard to hide them with makeup. But he wasn't worried, he had nothing to fear. Just like with the prostitute tonight, people had only seen Nina in the company of a lame, dark-haired, black-eyed man, casually dressed. And anyway, the last time he'd taken the same precautions with her as with Rosa. He had waited for Nina in the car, quite a way from Rue Saint Denis. No-one could claim that she had gone with him.

They went into the bedroom, and he let Rosa undress as usual, though tonight he wasn't going to need it, but he didn't want to arouse her suspicions.

'Did you bring the pills?'

'No. If the ones you have are the same, I'll take from yours. I already know the effect they have on me.'

He took the medication out of the bedside table drawer and showed it to the woman.

'You see they're the same. Shall I give you one or two?'

'One will be enough today, I'm dead tired.'

'Lie on the bed; I'll just go to the kitchen for a glass of water.'

He'd added a few drops of a sleeping drug to the water and the woman fell asleep immediately. Arbogast gave her the injection and went up to the lab to get the magnifying lamp and instruments to take samples. Before returning to the bedroom, he contemplated the workplace he'd set up so carefully for his research. It wasn't the money he was after from this artificial skin he'd been working on that was so different from the kind designed by his colleagues. His had nothing to do with what the rest were working on. He was working on creating liquid skin that was applied with extreme ease on any part of the body, with the help of a simple brush. It would then fuse with whatever fabric it was blended, leaving no trace. Nina and Rosa woke up after each session, without noticing or even suspecting that it had already merged with their own skin. And thus fused and invisible, that new skin began the work of rejuvenating the old. He had seen how Nina's skin became smoother as the applications advanced, first on the inside of her thighs, then on her belly, finally on her neck and face. His research was on the right track, of that he was sure, although something was still missing. Because Nina's skin had started to deteriorate in early May, almost a year after the first application; and then it split, as if it had been cut with a scalpel.

'What's wrong with your skin?' he had asked her the last night they had met to keep a record of any symptoms.

'See for yourself, these... these sores. On my face and body too.'

'Do you know what has produced them?'

'No idea. Some piece of shit that's infected me, I guess. It will pass.'

'Do they hurt?'

'What do you think?'

'Do they bleed?'

'No blood, just some kind of thick slime oozes out of them. Cream and makeup seem to stop it for a bit. It will eventually heal.'

'Have you been to see a doctor?'

'Not yet. You're asking so many questions! We only meet like this to sleep, so why does this matter so much to you? And if it does matter to you and you don't want me to stay, you'll have to pay for the whole night, and the taxi as well.'

The sores had taken about eleven months to appear. They were the first symptoms of rejection that were perhaps going to get worse and the become more conspicuous. He couldn't take any risks. And yet he was making good progress, he was sure. That's why he was going to interrupt his work for a while and then take it up again, after having analysed the samples he'd taken from Nina's body, and the ones he would take tonight from Rosa's.

He would work out what was going wrong and produce a skin that was going to revolutionise everything. No, it wasn't the money he was after, he had more than enough. Nor did he want to achieve the kind of success that some people call glory. No, what he wanted was something else. Success or glory are merely momentary, fleeting commotions, craved by the likes of sports people or artists. A scientist at the peak of his achievements receives respect, admiration and above all an acknowledgment from society that would owe him a permanent debt of gratitude. This kind of recognition was what he wanted and what he would get when his skin was ready. Soon, very soon.

He turned off the light in the lab and went back to the bedroom. The woman was already dead. He examined her skin with the magnifying glass. He had applied the first treatment at the beginning February, that was seven months ago. There were no signs of deterioration yet. On the contrary, the skin appeared smoother and plumper where he had intervened. He was on the right track, there was no doubt whatsoever. And perhaps in Rosa's case there wouldn't have been any sign of rejection. But he couldn't take the risk. Especially now. Elisabeth's skin had begun to show signs of deteriorating very early on, barely three months after the first application of the treatment, at the end of March. But she was an old woman, and these women who worked the streets were barely sixty years old.

He finished taking samples and wrapped the body in the quilt where it lay. Rosa had been a very slim woman, almost skinny, and he dragged her easily to the garden. He pushed aside the chairs and the plastic table he had bought to hide the excavation. He removed the tent pegs nailed at the four corners of the tarpaulin covered the ground, removed it and threw Rosa's body into the hole, on top of two other women, that he'd already covered with a layer of earth that was thick enough to prevent the stench from spreading. He filled the hole with the rest of the earth he'd set aside and kept covered over. Finally, he smoothed over the ground with the shovel, and put the garden table and chairs back where they belonged. Before long the place would be overgrown with grass again.

Once inside the house, he returned the magnifying glass and the samples to the laboratory and tidied up the bedroom. Once he'd removed his contact lenses, wig, clothes and the trainers covered in soil, and put everything in a garbage bag, he took a long shower.

*

Right from the start of the first consultation at the clinic, Elisabeth had asked him, 'Do something for my skin, doctor. Not so that I look younger, I already know perfectly well that that's impossible, and not even so that I seem not so old. I just want you to make it stay on my body, because it feels like it's getting loose and eventually it will fall off. It's as if it were no longer part of me.'

From the first consultation she had asked him, 'do something, whatever it takes', in that kind of demanding tone that doesn't take no for an answer. She had pushed him from the very beginning and even more insistently in recent months. *Do whatever it takes.* Although he had warned her that this treatment was still in the experimental phase.

'I've spent my whole life experimenting and trying new things, doctor. This isn't what's going to stop me now. I trust you. If you think it's going to work for me, I'll go with what you suggest.'

'But my treatment hasn't been approved yet, and therefore I'm not authorised to apply the new skin. It would be totally illegal.'

'At my age, that's not going to stop me either. But if what you want to tell me is that your fees will need be increased considerably, I also agree.'

'It's not a question of money.'

'Then what?'

'Of being cautious. You'd have to follow my advice meticulously. Without ever contravening it, in any way.'

'OK.'

'Follow it to the letter. Without ever deviating from what I advise you. Ever.'

She had accepted everything, keeping the treatment an absolute secret about from the people closest to her, using prepaid cards to talk on the phone so as not to leave any trace, the almost absolute secrecy of her visits to the clinic on the Rue des Mathurins where the treatment was administered. Nobody should know about this, and nobody ever did. Except for poor Valérie who, having left something at the clinic returned suddenly one afternoon and discovered Elisabeth lying on the treatment table.

Elisabeth had always respected his instructions, including the ones he gave her for Biarritz, an early morning appointment, in a modest apartment that he would suggest and that she should rent in her name. She had always followed his instructions.

So where did that strange man come from who'd just come to see him at the clinic?

'A friend, Madame Audiard, recommended I should come and see you.' But that wasn't true.

She had always kept her word. She would never have brought that man to him. So, who had? And what did that busybody know about his relationship with Elisabeth? But he shouldn't worry. Nobody could link him to the events in Biarritz or to women from the Saint Denis area going missing. And in any case no-one misses that kind of woman. 'They say she's gone away.' End of story. There was still the question of Valérie but he'd nothing to fear there if he acted calmly and intelligently. He'd call her on her mobile again as he had been doing regularly in recent weeks; and he'd also call her landline to leave another message on the answering machine.

'At least give me a call, Valérie, I need your help. The practice is chaotic without you, I just can't get organised.'

He finished dressing and left the garbage bag, which he had to get rid of, on the passenger seat of the car. Before leaving the house for good, he went back to the lab. He gazed around without turning on the light; it wasn't necessary. He knew that place perfectly well, like you know the itinerary of a trip you've always wanted to go on, the one you've been planning for a long, long time.

The garage door opened without a sound. The Rue Brillat-Savarin was still deserted. It was still dark.

*

The doctor was lying. Inspector Lavigne, of the Paris Serious Crime Squad, and Inspector Canonne, just arrived from Bayonne, were convinced.

'Proving it will be quite another story.'

'One way or another we'll manage, since he's lying.'

He was lying. The call he'd received to his mobile on 29th August did come from Valérie Riboust's phone, the police had already verified it. But it wasn't she who'd called. The doctor was lying when he said that he'd spoken on that occasion with his secretary. There was a good chance that, by that date, the woman had been dead for several weeks or was unable to communicate easily. The search that the police carried out at her home on Rue Pierre Larousse confirmed what the concierge had already confirmed – countless signs of a prolonged and unplanned absence, which had to include an answering machine full of unplayed messages, mostly from her boss begging her to call him because 'it's chaos without you'. Dr Arbogast had recorded his last message the day after Larten's visit to the clinic.

Valérie Riboust's cell phone had gone dead on 3rd July. There had been no activity from that point until the famous untraceable call to her boss on 29th August that had lasted for about two minutes, and then, once again, nothing. She hadn't used her credit card either during all that time, nor had she withdrawn money from any bank in any another way.

The doctor was lying. The police had gone to the Cochard clinic to question him. The white coat he was wearing emphasised the paleness of his face. He hadn't done much sunbathing that summer.

'We'd like to ask you a few questions,' Inspector Lavigne told him after being introduced.

'What's this about?'

'The disappearance of Valérie Riboust.'

'What do you mean disappearance?' Arbogast smiled, seeming to be fully relaxed. 'According to what she told me, she's on the Côte d'Azur.'

'Where exactly?

'I'm afraid I can't tell you because I don't know. She called me in a rush at the end of August, telling me that she'd found another job and just left. Immediately. A real disaster for me. I've been forced to close the Rue des Mathurins temporarily.'

'Did she call your mobile?' asked Canonne, who was beginning to understand why Larten had said the doctor was a good actor.

'Yes. The call must be registered there,' he answered, pointing to the mobile that was on his desk.

'Do you mean that you left a recorded voice message, or that you spoke with her?'

'I talked to her. She let me know very quickly what I've just told you, that she wouldn't be coming back to work in

ANTONIA LASSA

September. So she left immediately, a real disaster for...'

Inspector Lavigne interrupted him

'It's very important, doctor, are you sure it was her? Did you recognise her voice?'

'Perfectly. She's worked with me for several years. I recognised her instantly, as I just told you, Inspector.'

And yet he lied.

'If you don't mind, Lavigne said, we'd like to visit your office in the Rue des Mathurins.'

'I've already told you I've closed it temporarily.'

'Yes, but we'd like to go there, anyway. Maybe we can find something that might help us locate Madame Riboust.'

'If I were you, I'd look on the Côte d'Azur, in the office of some dermatologist or plastic surgeon.'

'We will, but we also want to visit yours. If you don't mind, of course. This isn't an official search.'

'Of course, I don't mind. You can go there whenever you like. Do I have to go with you? Because I'd rather give you the keys and let you go without me. I have a lot of work. I don't think you'll find much, though. Valérie took all her belongings. She literally emptied her desk.'

Now they had proof he was lying. Larten's testimony and the photographs he had taken from inside the dumpster.

'But I suppose,' said Canonne, 'that the files with your patients' details are still at the clinic.'

'Yes, the computer is still there. Open it and have a look at whatever you want. The access key is "mathurins". Something simple, very easy to remember even for someone as clumsy with computers as me. I'd rather give you the keys and you go without me. If you agree to that.'

'We agree, thank you,' Lavigne said, already knowing that they weren't going to find anything to help their investigation at that particular clinic. The doctor was giving them free and unfettered access to a totally empty place. Arbogast walked them to the door of his office. As Canonne said goodbye to the doctor with a handshake, he added, 'one more question,

100

doctor, if I may, when was Valérie Riboust's last day at work?'

'The last working day of June. I don't remember the exact date. In summer, I only go to the clinic if I have an appointment with a patient.'

'That means you give your secretary two months of paid vacation.'

'Yes.'

'Doesn't sound like a bad job, and yet she left.'

'The Cote d'Azur has more attractions, I guess,' replied the doctor smiling again, 'and certainly much better weather. Valérie must prefer the sun.'

'Although it's bad for the skin.'

'If proper precautions are taken it can be very beneficial.'

'But you prefer to avoid it. I mean you don't look like someone who has had a lot of sun this summer. May I ask where you spent the holidays?'

'I've spent the whole of August with my wife and my in-laws, at my in-laws' property near Rochefort. But you're right Inspector, I haven't had much sun. The main reason is that time just hasn't allowed it. And don't worry about the keys to the clinic, you can drop them in the mailbox there on the Rue Mathurins. I have several copies.'

As they had expected, the police found nothing of interest at Dr. Arbogast's clinic. Just an empty desk, an answering machine with no messages, and a computerised patient file, without the slightest trace of Madame Audiard.

But the doctor is lying, and once again, Canonne told himself, Larten is right.

He'd insisted on linking the two cases from the outset. The crime in Biarritz and the secretary's disappearance. And he was right again. Because the judge had just allowed Arbogast's phone to be tapped. And the decision to do so had been made, the Inspector was convinced, not so much because of Valérie Riboust's unexplained absence, but rather out of the possibility that the dermatologist had murdered Elisabeth Audiard.

The days passed and the surveillance of Dr. Arbogast didn't

provide the expected results. Just a few bland conversations with his patients, colleagues or friends; the same routine going between the flat on Avenue Georges Mandel and the clinic; and an occasional outing with his wife. The risk of more deaths was off, but the situation could drag on indefinitely, and Larten was growing impatient. He had parked his campervan in Bayonne and kept on calling and going in to see Inspector Canonne.

'You, here again. What an "expected" pleasure. Sit down, please.'

'Good morning, Inspector, I don't have to tell you why I'm here. Émile has to get out of jail now. You don't have the slightest shadow of an argument to keep him longer.'

Larten had put a woman's scarf around his neck and was wearing light make-up. And the Inspector thought his appearance was like a new bout of migraine. No matter how many you've had before, it always catches you off guard, as if it were the first time and you have to go back to the beginning. He took a deep breath and began massaging the back of his neck with his left hand.

'I need a little more time, Mr. Larten, I already told you.'

'Larten will do.'

'You can imagine that Arbogast is aware of Gassiat's arrest.'

'I have no doubt about that.'

'If we release the boy right away, Arbogast will find out and realise we also suspect him of the murder in Biarritz, and not just of his secretary's disappearance. And that's not in our best interest. Give me a little more time.'

'It is clear you're not the one in jail.'

'Gassiat is doing fine where he is, I guarantee. I've seen to it personally that he is.'

'Inspector, you're talking to me about the conditions he's being detained in. I'm talking to you about justice.'

'A little more time, that's all I ask of you. If Arbogast suspects that we've connected him with the murder of Madame Audiard, he's going take even greater care and not make the slightest mistake. And we have nothing solid against him. He has an alibi for the day of the crime, and the only thing we could contribute to the case of the secretary are the photos you took of the inside of the container, ordinary rubbish that anyone could've thrown away. We just need a little more time. We're looking for a place or a second residence for the doctor where the secretary, because she has to be somewhere, is either dead or alive.'

'I'm afraid she's already dead, by now.'

'Yes, unfortunately it's more than likely. But we need a little more of time. Arbogast will eventually make a mistake, everyone does.'

'If he's the kind of person that the murder seems to indicate, meticulous and calculating to the extreme, he won't make any mistakes. And even less so now that he knows the police are closing in on him.'

'We don't have anything else to go on. We have to wait for him to make that mistake.'

'He's not going to make a mistake now, I'm convinced. If we look for a mistake, what we should be assuming is that he's already made it. What I mean is, you have to focus on the past, not the future. What's his alibi for the day of the crime?'

'He was with his wife and in-laws on a property near Rochefort. He didn't move from there the whole month of August. All the members of his family will undoubtedly confirm this, and the mobile geolocation data also indicates this to be true.'

'How far is Rochefort from Biarritz?'

Canonne checked on his computer.

'About three hundred and fifty kilometres.'

'A little more than a four hours' drive, even if he avoided the motorways. At night there's hardly any traffic. Elisabeth Audiard was murdered in the early hours of the morning.'

'Around four.'

'It doesn't seem impossible to me that someone could leave Rochefort around ten-thirty or eleven at night, after making sure everyone is sound asleep. A doctor could easily get hold of strong sleeping pills, arrive in Biarritz, around three in the morning, commit the crime, and be back in Rochefort around eight in the morning, to be there for when everyone was waking up, perhaps a little later and a little more groggy than normal.'

'Let me check it out.'

It certainly wasn't impossible. Canonne consulted several route simulators on the internet.

'They all give the same estimate more or less, around four hours of travel, so it's a bit tight but it can be done between ten-thirty to eleven at night and eight to eight-thirty in the morning.'

'With a window of an hour or so in Biarritz for the murder and administering acid.'

'It's a bit tight but it can be done. And if that's what Arbogast did that night, he must have passed a security camera somewhere. Let's find out what car he used on holiday.'

'Please check all that as soon as possible, Inspector. Émile can't stay in jail.'

Larten had put them back on the right track. A grey Peugeot Tepee, driven by a man with dark hair and wearing sunglasses despite the time, had been filmed by the security camera of a service station on Route National 137. It had been heading north at 6.53am on 28th August. The car belonged to Evelyne Arbogast.

*

Larten was behind the wheel of his van when he received the expected call from Inspector Canonne. He activated the hands-free.

'Good afternoon, Larten, I'm calling to inform you that Gassiat will be out in a few minutes. Just as long as it takes to complete the last formalities.'

'Yes, I know Inspector. I'm driving to the jail to pick him up.

I'll take him to Arcachon myself.'

'And I also called to congratulate and thank you. I'm not going to pretend I'm unaware of how we're indebted to you in solving the crime in Biarritz and in Paris as well. Because he's killed three women there.'

'Yes, I'm aware of that.'

'Apparently Arbogast was trying to make an artificial skin and he used prostitutes as guinea pigs. As for the secretary, she had the misfortune of being an unwelcome witness to Elisabeth Audiard's visits to the surgery in the rue des Mathurins. He also used the old woman as a guinea pig.'

'And then he wanted to erase the fact that his treatment hadn't worked with acid.'

'He has cynically confessed that he killed those four women because the new skin hadn't worked, and he had to save his reputation and the future of his research. Anyway... he's already in jail, and Gassiat won't be long in coming out.'

'Yes, I've already parked in front of the prison and I'm waiting for him.'

'He won't be long.'

Larten had realised that Canonne hadn't called him to tell him what he already knew, but to tell him something he couldn't bring himself to say.

'Do you want to add anything else, Inspector?'

'I guess so, but I don't really know how.'

'Just try it.'

'It's to do with a woman who has left me and with a missing tooth, that both keep going around in my head... and telling me that I've been an idiot. Also, with you. What I wanted to tell you is that I don't know what my opinions are right now. But I do know that they're not the ones I had before. About almost anything. Not even on resin false teeth.'

'I'm happy for you, Inspector, and I also congratulate you.'

'Thank you.'

When Canonne hung up, Larten called Madame Duroudier, without deactivating the speakerphone.

ANTONIA LASSA

'Good afternoon Irène, I'm waiting for Émile in front of the prison. It won't take long for him come out.'

'Yes, they've lent him a phone and he's just called me. Do you know what he told me?'

'Something that has moved you, I can hear it in your voice.'

'Deeply. That he is afraid I will not want to see him again because of the *scandal* of this matter. And I have answered truthfully that I want to see him more than ever. What I haven't told him, because there are things that each one must learn for themselves, is that scandal sets us free, like those fires that bring new growth to the land they have razed. I haven't told him, because to understand how liberating scandal can be, you must be as old as I am.'

'You are many years old, Irène, but you are not old.'

'Sometimes I feel that way too, Larten, but never long enough to believe it.'

'You must believe it, because it's true. And now I have to leave you, they're opening the prison doors.'

'Many thanks, my friend. And don't forget that we still have some practical issues to sort out.'

'Don't worry about that now. I'll call you as soon as I get back to Paris in a few days.'

All the questions brought up by the case had already been answered. But for Larten there was a puzzle still to solve. What kind of emotion was it that drew him towards Émile Gassiat? Initially, during their first meetings, he'd called it curiosity. But it wasn't that. Curiosity is selfish, it only seeks self-satisfaction; it's all about what you can get. But what Larten felt for this young man was a generous emotion, one that wanted to give, allow, support. He didn't know what name to give that feeling yet, but it wasn't curiosity.

The prison door had just opened and Émile Gassiat appeared. Three weeks of being detained didn't show at all. He was dressed in his boating gear and looked like someone who had just stepped off his boat. Larten got out of the campervan to greet him. They shook hands.

'I'm going to open the back so you can put your things there.'

'Thank you. Your mobile office is so interesting. Irène has already told me about it.'

'It's perfect for me.'

'I can understand, yes.'

'Especially since you've also set up your recording studio somehow on a boat.'

'Yes, you're right, most of my compositions get started on the *Hirondelle*.'

They got in the truck and Larten started the engine.

'It's a funny name for a boat. I'd like you to tell me about it, we have a long way to go.'

'It's a small boat and it's many years old. My parents had already bought it second-hand before I was born, and they gave it the name, *Hirondelle*, just like those birds that are always flying, that never seem to land. Swallows.'

'Maybe they also thought of Flaubert.'

'Flaubert? I don't understand you.'

'*L'Hirondelle* is the name of the stagecoach that linked Yonville with Rouen, and that Emma Bovary took to leave her small-town life behind and attempt something bigger.'

'It's true, I'd forgotten. And it's a nice thing to say. Maybe my parents chose *Hirondelle* because of that too. A boat always takes you to something greater. And besides, my parents were great readers. But more than anything, *Hirondelle* is about their way of life, always moving from one place to another. My mother liked the sea, yet my father liked living inland. He repaired musical instruments for a living and said that the coastal climate wasn't good for them. So, they lived part of the week in a small farm they'd rented near Agen, and the rest of the time they went to Arcachon to spend time at sea on the *Hirondelle*. I've inherited the apartment they bought there and the boat. I gave up the farm. In that way I'm like my mother, I prefer the sea.'

'Which goes very well with your piano.'

'Perfectly. The sea is essential for my music. It's the basis of my compositions, at least for now. Maybe one day that will change. If you want, I'll email you some very short pieces so you can get an idea of what I'm looking for.'

'I'd love to hear them.'

'And to thank you also for getting me out of jail...'

'It's easy to defend someone who's innocent.'

'And especially because... for what's most important to me... I don't know how to express it in my own words, so I'm going to use Irène's. "Thank you Mr. Larten for having looked on me without contempt and without surprise."'

'I'm going to be very honest with you... and let's be on a first-name basis, Émile, I think we've earned it.'

'OK.'

'I feel something towards you that I refuse to simply call curiosity. But I don't know what other name to give this feeling. Perhaps *Hirondelle*, as well, because it goes round and round and searches inside me, and still can't find a place to land. But it's not curiosity. It's more to do with being willing. I'm ready now and I'll be ready in the future, to listen to what you want to tell me, to be your confidant if you have something to confide in me, to deal with your fears or your anxieties if you need reassuring. And to be there, simply, if you want to talk about your desire. I don't think you've talked much about these feelings.'

'No. Never, with anyone. Not even with them. I think that older people have a hard time putting words to some things, they prefer silence.'

Because silence keeps possibility alive, Larten thought. Nothing has been ruled out yet. And "still" is surely the most important adverb in old age.

'Elisabeth used to say that silence was an ally, just like the gloom in a bedroom that obscures marks and spots on our bodies.'

'You can talk to me now or in the future about these thoughts, if you want.'

'When I'm at sea, sometimes I say phrases out loud. I don't record them. I don't mix them with the sound of the sea. Not yet, but maybe one day. I've been thinking about it in jail. I'm not ready yet, but later I'd like to write an opera. Do you like opera?'

'Monique, my partner, likes it a lot, and I like to go with her and see her happy.'

'I think later my music will take that path. Joining together the sounds of nature with the human voice that is the most natural thing we have. A form of opera. I'm still not able to imagine it, but I want to do something like that. And when I'm on the boat sometimes I say phrases out loud, and some speak of my desire, as you say.'

'I would love to hear those phrases, as if they already belonged to one of your compositions.'

'You're right, I can see them like this. Like the text of a libretto, still very imperfect, very immature. But a script, which is no longer real life and therefore can be shared.'

'You can share it with me now or whenever. If you want.'

'Sometimes when I'm on the *Hirondelle*, surrounded by a completely black sea, without any points of reference, I say, for example, that because of my sexual preferences, I will be able to have lovers, even a wife, but that I'll never be able to have a girlfriend.'

'Why?'

'Because 'girlfriend' is a word that looks like a fruit that immediately degrades with time.'

Émile spoke slowly, calmly, without the slightest trace of sadness or tension in his voice. And yet Larten listened to him as if he were listening to someone scream, someone distressed with the same alarm or anguish.

'Have you ever been interested in someone your own age?'

'Yes, but it was... how should I put it...? Not enough.'

Traffic on the motorway was dense, challenging to drive in. Larten felt anxious, tense at the wheel. And he also felt a knot in his chest that wasn't caused by the traffic but by Émile's words that were now mixed with Mathilde's in his head, 'it's our bodies that age, not us.' And Larten was suddenly scared that Émile was living that phrase backwards, that his young body harboured a callously old-fashioned maturity that prevented him from being happy like young people are, with all their playfulness and confidence, not a care in the world.

'With girls my age it wasn't desire, it was... I don't know how to say it was... physical response. And certainly not planned.'

Larten had hardly known adolescence, he had been pushed very soon to adulthood by the awareness of his difference, of his being labelled as "other" He took his eyes off the road to take a quick look at the landscape, at the orderly, innocuous Landes pine forests.

But reaching a form of maturity so soon had not prevented him from being happy. He took several deep breaths to try to loosen the knot he felt in his chest.

'Everyone has their preferences, as you say, Émile, but that's not going to stop you from being happy. I know from experience. What you have to do is surround yourself with allies and teachers.'

Larten had had them – teachers of happiness, people who had generously got him started in appreciating the taste for life.

'Teachers of happiness, Émile, who show us how to recognise it when it's in us, and how to stir it up so that it chooses us.'

Émile was looking at him now with renewed attention. Larten felt it without seeing it because he kept his eyes fixed on the road.

'I didn't meet Elisabeth, but I have met Mathilde and Irène. And I think they're teachers of happiness for you because they're showing you with their attitude and with their choices that they defend and will defend their pleasure until the end.'

'Yes. And they teach me to defend mine. That's why I'd like to tell you how it all started, if you like.'

'Yes, I would.'

'Tell you about it as if it were written in a script that I'm reading to you.'

'OK.'

'We lived half the time near Agen. My father repaired musical instruments. My mother was a nurse who cared for people at home. She had many patients who lived in houses, farms, and also in the château owned by an aristocratic couple who had family, children and grandchildren, but who spent most of the year on their own. We started visiting them regularly because they would invite us over all the time. I think the man had fallen in love with my mother and for that reason he took care of me and was very kind to me.

'The baron treated us not only as equals, but as if we were members of his own family. But the baroness, an older, beautiful woman, made an effort to remind us with a multitude of small gestures, tones, looks, details that she added or suppressed, that they were great and we were small; that we were placed lower, much lower, on the social scale, and that in that house, despite the fact that her husband's extravagant behaviour might lead one to believe otherwise, this was not our place. I was a child. By myself I wouldn't have been able to understand what was happening. But later, as we drove home, my parents used to talk about all that. They gave a name to all that woman's gestures.'

'As if they subtitled them for you.'

'That's right; and I learned to observe those gestures carefully and to interpret them for myself. But I also learned another extremely important thing, not to bother about them, to even laugh at the situation. Because my parents laughed. They found the baroness's attitude, who always acted elegantly, amusing and inoffensive.

'*She puts her poison in a pretty bottle and presents it as perfume*, my parents would say, laughing, tolerating her behaviour. And so, although I could've grown up detesting that haughty woman, I didn't. I grew up, without knowing, doing the exact opposite, loving her or desiring her or both. And also understanding her contradictions, the poison of her jealousy or fear – my mother was beautiful and young – contained in the beautiful bottle of her dignity and elegance. Then the baron died, and we never went back to the château. I finished high school and enrolled at the Bordeaux Conservatory. And I thought I'd put all that in the past.'

Larten pulled off the highway. They were already very close to Arcachon. But he wanted to prolong the trip and listen to Émile's story until the end.

'Do you want us to stop for dinner before we arrive? You won't have anything to eat at home.'

'Thank you but I'd rather we go straight there. I'd like to go out on the water as soon as possible. And besides, I'm almost done with my story. Because a few years later, when my parents had already died and I was living alone, I went with a group of classmates to England, to a music festival.

'We stayed in the countryside, in one of those Victorian B&Bs. The owner was an older woman, an 'old woman' for us who were in our early twenties. I had already slept with girls my own age, but for this woman I felt a completely new desire. The clearest and most powerful I'd ever felt. She understood and saw it right away; I've already learned that older women easily perceive the desire they inspire in me even if I try to hide it...'

'You seem to also come with subtitles, then.'

Émile laughed and Larten felt the knot that had weighed on his chest for a long time finally loosen.

'Yes, and that woman knew how to read them very well and that night she invited me to her room. It was the first time I experienced real pleasure, although there had been pleasure at other times before. I don't know how to explain it.'

'I get it.'

'I felt the difference, the enormous difference. Probably because it was also the first time that I got intimately close to a body that bore the effects of life, powerful and at the same time vulnerable, beautiful and marked, trusting and sceptical. Generous and indifferent, because older people focus on people and things with a concentrated but restricted attention. That's the end of the story, Larten, or the beginning. This is what I desire, most probably since I was a child. I have desired this, I wanted it like this, in the most spontaneous and natural way in the world. Although it's so hard for people to understand or consider it without feeling mistrust or contempt towards me.'

Larten stopped the van in front of the small port of Aiguillon.

'People are never all people, Émile.'

'I know. Irene has also told me many times: "There are several billion people in the world; impossible for all of them to agree on something; thank goodness".'

'Yes, at least. Irene is someone who shows you what happiness is, just like Mathilde, don't forget that.'

'I won't. And I won't forget to send you the music either.'

They got out of the van and Larten handed him his things.

'Do you want me to help you carry them?'

'No, thanks, no need. I live right here. I'm going to take all this upstairs and then I'll go out in the boat.'

'Can you see it from here?'

'Yes.'

Émile pointed over at the illuminated dock.

'That little white one over there, look, you can make out the name.'

'Yes, I see it. *Hirondelle*. It's not big, but it takes you far.'

'That's what I'm trying to do. Like Emma Bovary; I'll remember that too.'

Larten stopped in the pine forest on the beach at La Teste-de-Buch. That night he would stay in the Bassin and sleep in the campervan.

He opened the small wine cellar and took out one of the bottles of Cahors that he had bought that same morning in Bayonne, from a winery, on the edge of the Adour, which he had liked very much. *Le sang des vignes*, he was going post about it on his blog. He uncorked the bottle, set it on the table, and turned on the computer. Tonight, he'd rather communicate with Monique by email; he didn't want another voice to dilute Émile's that was still echoing in his head: 'the voice is the most natural thing we have... older people offer an intense but limited attention to human beings and inanimate objects... the clearest and most powerful desire...'.

He exchanged some messages with Monique, checked his email and closed the computer.

He picked up a glass and poured himself three fingers of the Cosse-Maisonneuve to taste. And he thought of Émile's parents, experts in the art of using subtexts to teach their child to interpret the details, the small gestures, the cracks in the intonation.

He tilted the glass to evaluate the colour.

He had also had good teachers, who had instructed him in the art of happiness, of the taste for life, step by step, spelling it out for him, as in a tasting.

He swirled the glass and brought it to his nose.

It had been hard to identify the emotion Émile had stirred in him. Because it wasn't just curiosity or convenience. He saw it clearly now and in such a powerful way. It was also a form of desire. A desire that he had hardly ever experienced, that in the past he might have felt intensely but fleetingly. Just for an instant, after a particularly happy time with the woman he loved. But Émile had given him back that desire to be a parent; to become the teacher who, from the very beginning, shows you how to taste life, step by step, as wine is tasted, with the same care and the same fervour.

He brought the Malbec to his lips.